Everything Is a Little Broken

REBECCA SUGAR

Post Hill
PRESS

A POST HILL PRESS BOOK
ISBN: 979-8-88845-144-1
ISBN (eBook): 979-8-88845-145-8

Everything Is a Little Broken

Cover design by Jim Villaflores

This book is a work of fiction. People, places, events, and situations are the product of the author's imagination. Any resemblance to actual persons, living or dead, or historical events, is purely coincidental.

Post Hill Press
New York • Nashville
posthillpress.com

Published in the United States of America
1 2 3 4 5 6 7 8 9 10

For my father.

For my children so they will one day laugh with me when it is my turn.

For all my friends who have battled through their parents' old age and taught me so much about how difficult it is, and how brave they are.

And for myself, so I could bring Ella back for a time. It was wonderful to hear her voice again.

HOSPITAL HUMOR

MIRA SAT IN THE BACK seat of the car, looking out the window, on the ride up to Columbia Presbyterian Hospital. She pulled off her sunglasses to take in the unfiltered beauty of the tree covered cliffs running north along the shore on the other side of the Hudson River. The sun beamed across the water. "This is really the prettiest view in New York," she said aloud. "That land looks like it must have looked hundreds of years ago, truly unspoiled." Then she caught herself. "Of course, the water is polluted, but you wouldn't know it from looking. It's so inviting."

The driver glanced at her through the rear-view mirror. Mira realized then that she wasn't just talking to herself, so she returned his gaze and smiled.

"Is it really? Oh well, that's a shame," he answered politely. Then he seemed to consider her remark more carefully, and he shrugged. "Eh, you know, everything in life is a little broken, right?" He turned his attention back to the road.

She nodded and looked out the window again. "Yes, that sounds right."

Mira thought about her father. He had done well, her mother relayed, and was being moved to a private room. She was anxious to see him and dreading the sight of him at the same time.

The taxi pulled into the hospital's circular driveway and Mira remembered the last time she was there. Her father's first spinal cord surgery was thirty-five years earlier when she was just twelve years old. The night before the surgery, she walked to the hall linen closet to get a towel and saw him through the doorway to his room. He was sitting in his armchair, softly crying. It was the only time she had seen her father cry and it terrified her. Only much later would she understand that he wasn't crying for himself, but for her, her brother, and her mother.

The busy scene curbside was a sad one. Weakened people in wheelchairs had the look of the weight of the world on their faces and were being helped by teams of nurses and attendants kindly assisting them. Mira saw people pulling up in their cars, as opposed to the backs of ambulances, and decided that they were the lucky ones. A constant flow of traffic was being directed by a uniformed guard who smiled at everyone who passed by, and Mira smiled back in appreciation of him as she walked toward the door.

A rail-thin man sat on a bench near the hospital entrance, his elbow leaning on the armrest and his chin resting on his hand. He looked distant and defeated, as though he were reflecting on the horrible ordeal he had just endured, or perhaps contemplating the horrible ordeal awaiting him. Mira wasn't sure which it was. The expression on his face reminded her that the only lucky ones were the ones leaving, not arriving.

The scene inside was familiar as well. Thought and care had gone into designing the lobby. It was bright, with natural light pouring in, mercifully greeting its visitors with all the encouragement and optimism a pleasant environment can offer to those who find themselves in very unpleasant circumstances. Warm-colored couches and textured rugs defined cozy seating areas, and cheerful art covered the walls. Someone had decorated the space with compassion, wanting to offer beauty where ugly disease and infirmity resided for a time. Mira thought it was a truly admirable pursuit.

Against this backdrop, she recognized the slow shuffle of pale patients, fortunate enough to be on their feet, walking through the exhaustion and pain of each step. Escorting them were family members and friends, bearing another kind of pain written all over their faces. The ache in their eyes brutalized Mira as she passed by, but she never looked away. It felt cruel to let them know their suffering was unbearable to others.

In the elevator, a man balancing a cardboard tray of coffee in his left hand stood beside her. His right hand tapped nervously against his leg and Mira could hear him taking deep breaths. She wondered what he was bracing for. When the doors opened on the 9th floor, he rushed out.

She stepped into the hallway. The hospital designer clearly hadn't been hired to attend to the upper levels of the building. The walls were undecorated, painted in pale peach and beige. Signage signified the daily drumbeat of illness that passed through the corridors. Pediatric orthopedics this way. Oncology that way. The only sign in the building that bore any hope was the one that said "Exit." Mira focused on the room number she had been given and navigated her way toward it.

She opened the door slowly and saw her father lying on the bed. Matthew Frank was a proud man. Even after surgery at the age of seventy-nine, his silver hair was combed neatly, and he was wearing one of his blue business shirts over his gown. His collar was spread open, and his left sleeve had been cut from wrist to shoulder to make way for the many tubes attached to his arm.

Mira smiled, trying to imagine how he had managed to muscle his way past hospital protocol in post-op and get the nurses to put that shirt on him. He was surely pumped full of drugs, but his determination was obviously more powerful than the narcotics. She enjoyed the thought of the exasperated staff relenting to her father's wardrobe demands just to get him off their backs. It wasn't his vanity he was preserving; it was his dignity, and that was worth a struggle. And boy, could he put up a fight.

But he didn't look like a fighter now. He was pale. His skin seemed to sag around his eyes more than usual, as though his eyes were frowning in place of his mouth, which he contorted into a manufactured smile for the benefit of his daughter. Mira knew he would never let her see how much pain and fear he felt.

"Hi, Dad," she said firmly and brightly, just as she did any other day she saw him. It would have broken some silent rule between them if she had walked through the door weeping and fawning all over him. She didn't even have the urge to cry. There was a job to do.

Matt had been in chronic pain for decades as the result of a chiropractic injury that led to his first spinal cord surgery at the age of forty-four. The surgery saved him from full body paralysis but left him weakened. Every year as he aged, the compounding effects of his condition created new problems that deeply impacted his quality of life. He suffered atrophy, neuropathy, knee replacements and deteriorating discs until his physical limitations far outweighed his abilities and reordered his world.

But in every way that his body failed him, his expansive mind and courageous spirit compensated. His intellect was as strong as any of his attenuated muscles might have been, and his sense of humor was never dulled by his suffering. He refused to sedate himself with painkillers, unwilling to compromise his ability to run his business or to be fully present for his family. Most people looked at him and had no idea how much he struggled—all they saw was his strength. It was to that strength that Mira had clung since she was a child, and it was that strength she honored now by practically ignoring his latest run-in with the deterioration of his physical condition.

"You look amazing!" she said with a wry smile, walking toward him. Mira couldn't lift the physical weight off her father, but she tried to lighten the emotional one with her "as usual" banter. A little normalcy in less-than-normal situations, she had learned, was powerful medicine.

Approvingly, her father answered, "When you got it, you got it."

She moved a bit closer to the bed. "Nice shirt! Hospital-issue?"

"You should see what they tried to get me to wear."

His voice was still raspy, a result of the anesthesia and breathing tube used during the operation. Mira flinched a little when she heard it, hoping he hadn't noticed.

She looked over at the metal walker in the corner of the room. "Well, you never liked using that thing, but I bet you can't wait to jump back on it now."

"Jump?" he laughed at the thought. "The last time I jumped was probably 1963."

"I would have loved to have seen that—you catching air!" Mira wondered to herself if he knew what "catching air" meant.

"Catching what?" He had no idea.

"Don't worry Dad, you're not really old until they put those tennis balls on the bottom of your walker," she teased.

"Right, like those guys in the old age homes," he agreed, playing along.

"Leave it to you two to find the humor in a very unfunny situation." The voice came from the opposite corner of the room. Mira's mother had been standing there silently observing. She had almost no color in her cheeks, and her brown hair was limp and dry. That she was upright was perhaps the only indication that she wasn't the patient in recovery. Mira looked over at her to say hello.

"I am going to get a cup of tea," Dana Frank said. She nodded at her daughter and excused herself.

Mira turned back to her father. "She isn't a fan of hospital humor, I guess."

"No. She didn't even laugh when I asked the nurse if she would put some 'Tio Pepe' in my IV bag."

"Well, we're probably not as funny as we think we are," Mira acknowledged, moving closer to the bed. "But, it went well," she said getting more serious herself. "Yes, the doctor was happy," he answered.

She raised an eyebrow. "And you?"

Matt lifted his arms one inch off the mattress and looked directly at his daughter. "I am happy not to be paralyzed, yes," he said, "but this isn't what I was expecting from a *successful* outcome."

Mira's mother had texted her the details supplied by the doctor while Matt was still in recovery. The surgery was successful, but it left a certain percentage of its patients with temporarily decreased mobility in their arms. Matt woke up with no movement at all. It was yet another blow, meted out to someone who had a lot of experience taking them.

"It has only been a few hours and you already have some movement coming back, Dad. The doctors say…" Mira began, but he cut her off.

"Yes, I know what they say. They say I will regain mobility with time. But they aren't sure how much, or when. They told me to be patient, but as you know, patience isn't exactly my calling card."

"No kidding," she replied, knowingly. "At least the scar is smaller and will heal quickly."

"Maybe. At my age you don't bounce like you used to."

"You will regain your strength," Mira said with conviction. "It will take a few weeks or months, and it won't be fun, but you will."

He scoffed. "Strength? At the moment, I am just hoping to be able to buckle my own belt again. Strength isn't even on my wish list. And did you say fun? You will have to define that word for me, because my last recollection of having any is hazy. Either way, I wasn't counting on having fun."

"Oh, for God's sake, please just let me be a cheerleader for thirty seconds," Mira said sighing, wondering why she thought he would ever have tolerated that approach. "Look…" she began, but her father cut her off again. Suddenly, he had a playful look on his face.

"What's that song? I think it's an old Broadway song—*Are You Havin' Any Fun*—do you know it?"

"Huh? No, never heard of it."

Matt began to sing. "*Better have a little fun / You ain't gonna live forever / So, while you're young and gay, still ok / Have a little fun!*" He was very pleased with himself. "There is more, I just have to remember the words."

"Okay, okay. Don't start up again. I beg of you. I am glad you are in the singing mood, but I don't need to hear anymore. You aren't exactly Chris Stapleton."

"Chris who...?" he laughed. "I don't know who that is, but I will have you know that in my day I was known for my voice. Women swooned."

"Never mind." Mira shook her head lovingly, sympathizing with his nurses. It was quiet for a few seconds before she spoke again. "It isn't great that this happened, Dad—"

"But it happened," he said completing her sentence.

"Yes, it did," she agreed, "and now we are going to have to figure it out."

Matt nodded. "Listen, I don't expect to run a marathon, or to start playing the piano. But I would like to be able to get out of this bed without help, and maybe sign myself out at the front desk. That doesn't seem unreasonable, does it?"

"Of course not," Mira softly replied, silently wishing her father's expectations for recovery didn't have to be so modest.

"Anyway, I'm determined to do what it takes to get back as much movement as I can so I can return to my normal, broken down, malfunctioning self. I can't stay like this. All these years, I never really saw myself as "handicapped" but now..."

It was Mira's turn to interrupt. "Now? Dad, seriously, the Department of Motor Vehicles sent you that blue car-tag with the white outline of a man in a wheelchair six years ago. It's called 'handicapped parking' for a reason. You may have refused to use your wheelchair all this time, but that doesn't mean you didn't need it." She waited for his reaction, hoping she hadn't gone too far too soon.

Thankfully, he smiled. "Yes, well, it was nice knowing I could park anywhere, but I always felt fraudulent using that tag. Handicapped is a big word. I always thought of myself as a man with a bad back and some bad luck," he said.

"Well, you did have both of those," Mira agreed, understanding his resistance to the label. "Anyway, if it makes you feel better, I don't think people say "handicapped" anymore. We can call you "disabled" if you prefer it."

"Those are my choices?"

She looked at him lying in bed. She had always thought of him as physically disabled. The early-onset arthritis that led him to the chiropractor who caused his injury had always limited his movement. She had one memory of him in the ocean on a family vacation in Cape Cod when she was nine. He couldn't swim even then. But he could wade into the water waist deep and balance against the gentle waves by himself. That was unthinkable now. Her memories of her father were not of skiing vacations or throwing balls in the yard. If she thought about it, she realized she had never seen him run.

"Well," Mira continued, realizing that starting up again was what they both needed, "we will just push you around in a wheelchair until you get your strength back, and then you, your walker, and I can go for strolls around your block like we used to. The good old days! You will be back to racking up those five hundred steps a day like the senior citizen athlete you truly are."

Matt peered up over his glasses at his daughter. "What do you think the chances are of me getting into a wheelchair and letting you push me around the streets of Manhattan?" he asked. She didn't have to answer that question.

"As for walking, I am game, but it took me forty-five minutes to loop around the block with you before. Now you will have to schedule your whole day around dragging my old body down the street."

"Maybe if I chase you with the wheelchair, that will inspire you to move a little faster," she joked. He didn't offer a clever retort.

Walking around the city had become risky business for Matt over the years. Mira had never noticed how broken up and uneven the sidewalks were. With her new eyes adjusted to her father's condition, she realized they were an invitation to those unsteady on their feet to land on their backs. She pitied old people in New York, struggling to make it through the crosswalk before the light changed, or carrying a heavy grocery bag on pavement riddled with large cracks. The whole world seemed like an obstacle course.

Wanting to change the subject, she grabbed one of the five newspapers that littered the end of her father's hospital bed and sat in the chair near the window. "Another attack in the subway," she reported, having scanned the front page. "Looking out the window at this view of the river, you would never think the city is imploding."

Matt seemed distant in his response. "What is happening to this world?" he wondered, almost to himself. Then his eyes set on his daughter. "I worry about you. This may not be a safe place for you in twenty years." He had been saying this a lot lately. "I won't be here, but you and Aaron will, and Lilly!" He loved his granddaughter. She was his only grandchild, which he reminded Mira of endlessly.

She knew then that it was a mistake to bring up the state of the world. Her father felt assaulted by it on a good day. Matt's world was, for the time being, the hospital room he inhabited, and he needed to focus his energies there so he could go home as soon as possible.

"What do you mean you won't be here?" she asked, waving her hand dismissively. "With your luck, you'll actually live to one hundred and twenty."

"Don't wish that on me," came the reply. "Who wants to live that long? I can't afford it!" he continued, starting to smile.

This conversation had become scripted between them over the years. Mira liked their routines, even if the subject matter wasn't ideal at the moment. She hoped the rhythm of their usual banter would relieve some of her father's anxiety, as well as her own.

"You pickle yourself with Aqua Velva," Mira laughed. "It's a preservative. You will outlive us all."

"Well, if I have to hang around, at least I will smell fresh and clean." They were interrupted by breaking news on the television that hung from the corner of the room. An eighty-seven-year-old woman was attacked in broad daylight on the Upper East Side. They were looking for the man who punched her to the ground. Mira couldn't catch a break.

"Animals," Matt said.

She could see the pain on his face. His laments about the state of the world used to come and go, but over the last couple of years, something had changed. Lately, she felt her father's physical ailments had joined forces with the general fragilities of old age to create a new kind of vulnerability in him.

"What is happening to this world?" he repeated, not expecting an answer.

Mira reached over, grabbed the remote, and pushed the mute button. "This isn't news, it's noise," she said dismissively.

"But it's real," Matt replied. "You can't ignore it."

"Watch me! It may be real, but so are our problems and I would rather concentrate on fixing those." Mira couldn't make eye contact with her father as she spoke. They both knew there was no great "fix" in their future. So, she changed the subject—again.

She drew a pocket-sized binder of photos out of her bag and pulled her chair over, close to him. "We got the proofs back from the birthday dinner," she said, holding them up so he could see. His face lit up. It worked.

"I can't believe this was five months ago," she said as she huddled close to him. "It feels like a lifetime ago."

Together, they looked at the pictures as Mira turned the pages slowly. "Oh, that's a nice one of Dr. Baron," Matt said. Mira studied her father's face in the shot. He was smiling at his old friend, but wincing slightly, and she noticed.

She had organized everything for his comfort that night: the removal of uneven carpet on the floors that might catch under his walker, the placement of a chair with arms at the corner of the large family dinner table so he could maneuver in and out, having him arrive early so he could be seated and tuck the walker away in the corner where no one would witness him using it.

Despite all her preparations, he had still suffered. The pain that ran up his leg and through his back worsened the longer he sat in the same position.

The suffering momentarily retreated into the background, however, when Lilly stood up to make a toast. Mira remembered the joy overwhelming the anguish, even if just temporarily. Few things served as a salve to Matt Frank's pain like the pleasure of being with his granddaughter.

"Remember Lilly's toast?" Mira asked, smiling, flipping through the pictures to arrive at the ones of her daughter. "I can't believe she had the courage to sing that song in front of everyone!" she said, prompting her father.

"What do you mean courage?!" Matt asked, pretending not to understand. "What is wrong with that song? It is a classic!" Then he began to sing, "*Oh they don't wear pants on the sunny side of France, but they do use grasses to cover up their a****!*" Mira mouthed the words along with him. "I was taught that song by my uncle when I was a child, and I passed it on to you and my grandchild. It's a Frank family hymn," he insisted.

Mira smiled. "At least she bleeped the last word," she said, remembering.

"Honestly, it isn't even kind of the worst thing you have taught her," she continued, laughing as she reminded him of all the songs, poems, and life lessons he had imparted to Lilly from the time she could speak. "That girl got quite the education sitting at your Friday night dinner table for eighteen years. College is probably a lot less shocking than it would be otherwise."

From the look on her father's face, she could see how happy this made him. "Well, at least I know I have made an impression on her. She will never remember me as some generic grandparent, but as the grandpa who taught her the good stuff."

"No one would ever accuse you of being generic," she assured him. "Remember when Daniel got up and started singing 'Nobody Likes Me, Everybody Hates Me, I'm Gonna Eat Some Worms' with her?"

"That was always his favorite." The wrinkles of joy around Matt's eyes softened as he thought about his son. That Daniel flew in for the occasion was an unexpected, but happy, surprise.

Mira found a picture of her brother performing that night. He was clutching a microphone with one hand and a scotch with the other. His mouth was open wide, and he looked almost like the carefree, happy child she once knew. Together, she and her father stared at the photo in silent reflection.

The reminiscing was interrupted when Matt moved his arm slightly in a failed attempt to reach out and touch the picture. He bumped the table next to his hospital bed, knocking over the glass of water resting on it. Mira rushed over with paper towels to clean the mess quickly, trying to erase evidence that it had happened in the first place.

"We have to get you one of those long grabbers," she said, kneeling on the floor, still cleaning. "I know I have seen them on infomercials." Matt just grunted, unable to laugh along.

"I never thought I would ever buy anything on an infomercial. Look what you have turned me into," she joked, still wiping.

She looked up at her father. It wasn't fear she saw in his eyes. She thought it might be resignation. That was worse.

About a month before the surgery, an envelope was delivered to Mira's apartment. Matt had written his daughter a long, handwritten letter asking her to make hard decisions on his behalf if things went badly. This surgery wasn't at all likely to result in any such decision, but he wasn't taking any chances. He never did. He worried around corners, soothed by the thought that he had prepared for what might go wrong in advance of it happening. Then if it did, he wouldn't be delayed in contending with the problem by any need to wrestle with things like shock.

The Friday night after the letter arrived, he pulled his daughter aside at dinner and asked her to commit. "If I come out of this surgery paralyzed from the neck down…" he started, but Mira wouldn't let him finish.

"Oh seriously," she interrupted him, "stop! You know the chances of that are about one in a million."

"Exactly my odds. Mira, if that happens, I don't want to live that way."

She rolled her eyes. "Fine, I promise to hit you over the head with a frying pan if that happens, okay? Twice if the first blow doesn't do the trick."

Mira could see that he was satisfied. It was easy to imagine that she could conjure up the courage to crush a bottle of pills into his applesauce to spare him the indignities of a life he didn't want to live. But it was less easy to imagine how that decision would torment her after she made it.

She looked at her father now with his limp arms and useless hands in the hospital bed, and the chill that was running up his spine ran up hers as well. His worst nightmare was to be helpless, and it was hers as well.

PRAISE THE LORD

JUST THEN, DANA RETURNED TO the room and had her phone stretched out in her hand as she approached the bedside. "Matt, Mae is on the phone for you," she said as she placed the phone to his ear and held it there.

Mae was ninety-four years old and one of the few people on the planet who held authority over Mira's father. She had been his nanny since childhood when she started working for his parents at the age of twenty. She stayed with the family as Matt grew, left for college, and got married, and then she came to live with Matt's own family to take care of Mira and Daniel.

"Matthew," came Mae's aged voice over the line, "you there?"

"Yes ma'am, still kickin'."

When he spoke to Mae, he adopted her tone and vocabulary. They had a shared language, like a verbal dance between old friends.

Mae stopped working twelve years earlier only at Matt's insistence. She spent her time at church or at home watching her beloved baseball games. She was a true Mets fan. Matt paid her expenses and spoke to her daily. He used to visit her once a week, but she lived on the third floor of a walk-up building, and it quickly became impossible for him to get up the stairs. He started sending a car to bring her to their apartment once a month for visits, but eventually, Mae couldn't get down the stairs, and the visits stopped. Still, the bond between them was as strong as ever. Even now, as Mae lay bedridden in her apartment in Brooklyn, half-blind and fragile, she was a guiding force and source of comfort to him.

Mira could hear the whole conversation because both Mae and her father were hard of hearing and speaking at full volume. "Dad, you are yelling. Your voice isn't even fully recovered. Where is your hearing aid?"

Matt waved his hand dismissively. "I can never remember to charge the damn thing."

"You remember everything," she answered him sharply. "You just can't admit that you need it, but the poor guy in the next room can clearly hear that you do."

Matt looked at her and then gestured toward Dana. "If you had to live with your mother, you'd take it out too. It is so much more pleasant when you can't hear your wife yelling at you."

"I wonder if anesthesia turns all old, white, Jewish men into Jackie Mason..." Mira teased him.

He ignored the comment and turned his attention back to the phone. Dana barely reacted. She had a routine with Matt as well.

"Praise the Lord," Mae said louder. "You've got to praise Him, thank Him for what He do," she said. Matt accepted the instruction with an even louder "Yes, ma'am," although at the moment he had to work hard to find the praise in him.

"Mae, they tell me I may not get full use of my arms back," he said a little sadly, almost like a child talking to a mother who would feel his pain even more acutely than he did. And Mae did. She suffered along with him through every challenge of his life. He told her all his troubles, without fear of sounding like he was complaining. He could tell her about the weight of the world because she understood what life's weight felt like better than most.

"The Lord is going to touch your body," Mae said with prophetic emphasis, as though she were speaking to Him at that very moment. She repeated her prayer again and again—"He will touch you. He will touch your body and heal you!"

For Mae, the line between dialogue and prayer was often blurred. Everything she said was suffused with her faith. It didn't matter if those were the Lord's words or not. They soothed Matt, as they had all his life when his body betrayed him, and Mae prayed over him. His pain was hers and knowing that did heal him in a way. It occurred to Mira just then to use her phone to record the conversation between them. She sensed she would want to hear it again one day.

When Mira was young, she remembered Mae praying over her when she was sick. She was prone to strep throat with high fevers and Mae would stand over her bed with a washcloth soaked in rubbing alcohol and wipe her skin down to cool it. All the while she spoke in tongues, invoking whatever spiritual power she communed with. The jumbled sounds were uttered with such forceful intention that Mira thought they might be actual spells that would break her fever. Mae spoke them like a master defense attorney coaxing a favorable ruling from a jury. She had no real power in this world, but when she called on her God to do something for someone she loved, she seemed omnipotent.

Thinking back on it, Mira smiled. She was a Jewish girl on the Upper East Side with a Pentecostal, black woman intoning indecipherable incantations over her, laying hands on her body to pull the sickness out of her. Her father would stand there too, which made the scene even more ridiculous—he, with his deep, traditional Jewish faith, his Ivy League degree, and rational businessman's mind. But it wasn't ridiculous. They were more than their labels suggested. They were friends, fellow travelers, and prayer partners, calling forth healing like two ancestral elders from another time and place. *How great it would be to have a video of that to watch over and over again*, she thought.

Mira listened to her father speaking to Mae and thought that relationships like theirs were relics of another world, the sort that were fading into history and would never be again. Maybe that was as it should be, she told herself, but it still saddened her.

~ ~ ~

Dana propped the phone up on a stand on the side table, placed it on speaker, and motioned to her daughter to come outside the room with her for a moment. Mira had wanted to talk to Mae herself but saw the urgency on her mother's face, so she followed her out the door as her father continued his conversation.

"Mira," began Dana, who was looking somewhere between her daughter's shoulder and chin though they only stood two feet apart, "Dad will be going home in a few days, and he needs a lot of help. Physical therapy every day and around-the-clock, in-home nursing. He can't get in and out of a chair, get dressed, or take a shower until his arms are working fully again. He is going to fight me on hiring people, so I need you to help convince him."

She was matter-of-fact in her description, devoid of any sign of emotion as usual. She had never been the warm, effusive type. When Mira was a child, it bothered and confused her. Later in life, she began to understand that it wasn't that her mother lacked human emotion; it was that she suffered enormously from it. She couldn't show any of it, or all of it might come pouring out. Mira had come to accept that much in the same way she had never seen her father run, she had never seen her mother belly laugh. Each parent had his or her limited capacities, she concluded.

Dana knew her daughter could talk her husband into doing what was best for him in a way she could not, and she used this when she needed to. Mira knew her mother hated to ask. But she was right—her father did need a lot of help, and her mother couldn't handle him alone and would never be able to persuade him like she could.

"Sure, okay," Mira replied. Neither woman made direct eye contact with one another, but they both knew the matter was settled.

There was an awkward pause and Mira thought she saw her mother move slightly toward her. Reflexively, she tensed up and remained still. She and her mother never hugged. The two women quickly turned away from each other and went back to the room. Mira suddenly became aware that she hadn't asked her mother how she was holding up. A flash of shame rushed through her, but she still didn't ask. She wasn't sure why.

~ ~ ~

Mae and her father had already finished talking. The news was still on, and Matt was fixated on it. Mira had forgotten there were streaming closed captions at the bottom of the screen, and her father was reading along with the bad news of the day. *Forty people shot in Chicago this weekend,* the newscaster robotically reported. She could see her father absorbing the chaos of a city he didn't even live in and hadn't visited for years.

His nature was to worry. It was like a switch he couldn't turn off in a world that increasingly grew more treacherous and threatening as he grew older. The cruelty of this burden was that he couldn't release it because that would only make him worry more. Sometimes Mira believed that the enormous amount of energy generated by her father's chronic, churning anxiety substituted for his lack of physical power and was the very thing that kept his poor old body from collapsing altogether, and so it served him.

She sat in the chair next to his hospital bed again and began to feel overwhelmed. It had been happening a lot lately, but she pushed it aside, afraid the feeling would show on her face and add to her parents' woes. "Mae sounded like…Mae," she said, conjuring up a bright and cheery tone of voice. "How many 'Praise the Lord's' did you count during that brief call?"

Matt smiled and moved his fingers slightly along the bed sheets. "I couldn't count."

When he spoke about Mae, there was a compelling look of both sadness and joy on his face. Mira understood that look. It was the look of someone who knew that he was on the precipice of losing one of the most important people in his world. Mae was a touchstone of life for Matt—she knew his childhood friends, his parents, his college roommate. She had been there when he started first grade, when he got married, and when Mira got married too. She was the one person left on earth who knew his whole history, and he couldn't know how much longer she would be with him.

"How is she feeling?" Mira asked.

"She said she is fine. But she always says that, even when she isn't. You know how she is."

As a child, Mira loved Mae like a grandmother. She knew nothing of her life outside of the Frank home, and it didn't often occur to her that she might have one. On Friday nights, after the Sabbath dinner, she would race upstairs to Mae's room and jump under the covers of the empty twin bed across from hers. She would steal the remote control and switch from the Mets game to *Dallas*, laughing off Mae's half-hearted protests. She was a constant and beloved presence, and it was impossible to imagine her as a part of anyone else's family.

Only later did Mira start to hear stories about Mae's husband who died just a few years after their son, Joseph, was born. That was when she started working for the Franks. She cooked and cleaned and tended to their family, and as a result, she spent a lot of time away from her own. Joseph died at seventeen of a drug overdose. Mae never talked about him with Mira, but Matt had once told her that had he lived, Joseph could have been a Hollywood actor—he was exceptionally handsome and full of charm. Mae kept a small photo of him in the back cover of her Bible.

"What a pair you two are," Mira mused, looking at her father. "I can just picture Mae there in Brooklyn, in her long aqua blue nightdress, praising the Lord. And here you are in your hospital gown with your business shirt on, doing your Matt routine. Other than the fact that both of you are currently bedridden, nothing has really changed."

Matt was still smiling. "She loves blue, that's for sure. I don't think I have ever seen her in another color, now that I think about it. Blue nightgown, blue work dress, blue holiday dress.

Remember how you used to tease her that you were going to buy her a pink, feathered negligee just to change things up?"

"Right, like I used to tease you that I would buy you a pair of jeans. Equally ridiculous. I don't even know if she knew what a pink feathered negligee was. She used to laugh and say, 'What are you stuttin' 'bout, girl?' I never found out what 'stuttin'' actually meant, but it was always one of my favorite words."

"Mine too," Matt agreed. "Anyway, Mae told me that the Lord is going to give me strength back in my arms."

"Well, while the Lord is at it, maybe he should also make you thirty pounds lighter," Mira suggested with a grin.

Dana jumped in. "That would take more than an act of God. Maybe He can just chip in with fifteen pounds."

Matt and Mira looked at her approvingly.

Then Mira turned back to her father and to the subject of Mae's pronouncement. "Well, that's good news because we all know Mae is a prophet," she said. "She definitely has a direct line to the divine. If He were going to choose anyone to speak to, it would be her. She would never use the connection to complain or ask for a winning lottery ticket. She would be an ideal human transmitter for any deity—humble, grateful and ready to receive. And I wouldn't want to get in her way when she is speaking for Him."

"That's so true. He *would* choose her," Matt agreed. "Look at her life. She has so much to complain about but never does. She does the opposite; she was always grateful to God for every little thing. She worked so hard. You know what I remember, Mira? When I was young, there were no laundry machines. Mae would wash all the clothes and the linens by hand and then haul the laundry down to the basement of our building in a large, heavy basket. There was a big room filled with steam, and she would pin each piece of clothing to a line that she pulled through that room. Then she carried everything up to the apartment and ironed for hours with her Bible open next to her. It was hard labor. She was on her feet all day."

"You know, some things about 'the good old days' weren't really that good," Mira mused. "Life before washing machines doesn't sound great."

"It was another world," Matt replied both nostalgically and with acceptance. "Mae endured so much—more than just hard work. And she always had unshakable faith. She is a force of nature."

That kind of faith was appealing to Mira, but she couldn't access it herself. In her early thirties, her friend had taken her to a Kabbalist in Brooklyn who met with her for twenty minutes and spoke to her compellingly about her soul's purpose. He gave her some papers to take home with instructions to read them every day for forty-five days. On each page were letter formations in transliterated Hebrew. She was instructed to scan them, but not read them aloud as though they were words. They were Kabbalistic representations of the various names of God.

Try as she might, she couldn't resist the urge to try to read the letters and turn them into words that made sense. She understood that the mystical idea was that the letters themselves had energy and that any attempt to organize and control them was to defeat the purpose of the exercise. But she couldn't stop herself. She didn't have Mae's ability to surrender and connect, so she gave up after just four days.

The nurse came in and spoke cheerfully. "Hello again! How has your day been so far, Mr. Frank? Good?"

"Good? I've had better," he answered. She giggled and shook her head.

Matt nodded toward Mira. "This is my daughter, Mira Cayne," he said. "Mira, this lovely nurse, Alice, was here earlier and yelled at me just like you did for not using my hearing aid. I told her that a handsome older gentleman such as myself could not wear something as unattractive as a hearing aid and ruin her perfect view whenever she entered the room."

"And I told him that the same comment by a healthy, upright man would get him 'Me-Too-d' in another setting," the nurse shot back, smirking, addressing Mira as though she already knew her.

"That didn't scare me, I already had a catheter inserted so nothing they could do to me could be worse," he volleyed back.

Alice had a good sense of humor and twenty years on the job, so Matt didn't faze her. She said she was back to check in on him and see if he was comfortable. Big mistake.

"Comfortable?" Matt said, a mischievous smile on his face. "I haven't been comfortable for thirty-five years! You're a little late," he admonished her. "And if I say I am not comfortable, what are you going to do? Tickle my back and sing to me?" He was on a roll. Mira could see life coming back into his drawn face as he bantered with Alice. Alice could see it too, and, in her kindness, she just let him continue.

"I would be more comfortable if I could dance a ballet. Have a tutu handy?" Now he needed a reaction, so he paused, and she gave him one.

"I have never seen a tutu in your size, Mr. Frank, but I will see what we have at the front desk." Bingo. She gave the patient what he wanted. He was delighted.

He did have one request. He asked Alice for something to help with the dryness in his lips.

"I have some balm I can give you," she offered.

"Balm? What is b-a-l-m?" he repeated, pronouncing each letter of the word as though it were foreign to him. He was having another go. This was classic Matt Frank. Just when you thought he was spent, there was more left in him. Mira just sat back and enjoyed the show.

"Balm," Alice explained, "like Vaseline."

He grimaced. "Oh, not Vaseline," he replied. "I don't like all that greasy stuff on my skin. I definitely don't want Vaseline."

Alice tried to explain that balm was thicker than Vaseline and wouldn't get all over his face—just his lips.

"No, I don't want that. It's too greasy," he answered.

"Well, what do you want?" she asked with resignation, a twinkle in her eye.

"You're the nurse!" he exclaimed. "You don't know what to get a patient for dry lips? Aren't 'lips' in week one of nursing school? Oh boy, you should get a refund. You don't know what soothes dry lips?"

Alice didn't bother to answer. She just waved her hand at him and left the room. Mira attempted to shoot the fleeing nurse a knowing glance. Dana didn't even move. After fifty-three years of marriage, this was white noise and she ignored it entirely.

Matt was enjoying the moment when Alice walked back in. "Here," she said as she drew a ChapStick from her pocket.

"Ah!" he exclaimed. "Now *this* is a nurse," he said, nodding toward Alice. "She brought me a ChapStick! *This* is medicine for dry lips! Finally. Here, help me put it on," he asked her.

She obliged and with a wry smile of her own, said, "Mr. Frank, do you know what we call ChapStick where I come from?"

He was intrigued. "What?"

"Lip b-a-l-m," she replied flatly. She turned, triumphant, and left. Matt didn't even have a quick retort. Mira and her mother were impressed. With nurses like these, he would get better faster. Maybe it was his strategy. If he drove everyone mad, they would work twice as hard to get him discharged.

~ ~ ~

The next day, Mira arrived at the hospital earlier than expected. When she entered her father's room, it was eerily quiet. Her mother was out. He was asleep, propped upright in the hospital bed, his head tilted slightly toward the window. The light streaming in highlighted the absence of color in his face. His mouth hung open a bit and he was completely still.

She could hear the machines attached to her father beeping confirmation of his pulse, but she froze in place for a moment, acknowledging that this view of him would one day be a much more unhappy one. She prayed that day would be years away, but as they both aged, the reality that those years were shorter in number than they used to be hit her differently. Seeing him this way made it all feel more imminent and she shuddered.

So many people depended on her father. What in the world would they do when he wasn't here anymore? What would she do? She shuddered again.

Mira stood near the doorway watching him sleep, not wanting to disturb him. He so rarely got any rest.

A few minutes later, he opened his eyes slowly and turned toward her and smiled. "Hello dear," he eked out. "How are you?"

He was really exhausted today. She could tell by the movement of his head, which he struggled to tilt in her direction, and by the slurring of his words. The pain medicine must have made him groggy. But he was pushing himself to attend to her, still taking care of her even now. He was still the parent. And she liked that he was.

"Me? I'm fine. I didn't just have surgery," Mira answered him. "How are *you*?"

"Never better," he said weakly, trying but failing to gesticulate with his limp arms. His lips looked dry, and his voice was weak, but he had the old look in his eyes of someone fighting his way back rather than retreating into himself. That look reassured her.

"That's great!" she replied, forcing a smile. "You will be home tomorrow and the road to real recovery begins."

He looked at his daughter. "I will do what I can," he assured her.

She knew he would, and so would she.

THANK GOD FOR GLORIA

THE NEXT MORNING, MATT WAS discharged. Dana arrived early to take him home.

"I am getting out of here before they change their minds," he told Mira over the phone.

"Oh, don't worry. I'm sure they can't wait to see you off. Alice is probably holding the door."

"You mean barring it! She's going to miss me; I know it," he playfully insisted.

"You sound ready. That's good."

"You should always be ready to leave a hospital, Mira. Long stays in places like this are to be avoided."

"Agreed. Maybe try avoiding them altogether in the future, okay?" she suggested.

"Why didn't I think of that?"

She called the apartment to check in on him again a few hours later, and Gloria, the home health aide her parents had hired, answered the phone. She reported that Matt was doing his exercises and that Dana had gone to lay down, but not to worry—it had all gone smoothly. Mira was running late for a board meeting, so she left a message that she would be over later in the day.

She jumped into a cab and placed her phone in her lap, just in case they called. The taxi wended its way down Park Avenue, hitting every pothole and crack in the pavement. "Gotta love New York!" she said aloud. "This must be what riding on the back of a horse and buggy felt like." The driver didn't respond.

She tried to mute the ad screen several times, but the button wasn't working. To her left, she spied a wad of crumpled, used tissues pushed into the seam of the seat, and an empty water bottle rolled around on the floor. Mira was done. "I will jump out here," she said, preferring to walk the last few blocks.

As she rushed down the sidewalk, she avoided the bare-chested homeless man stumbling across the pavement barking at pedestrians. Sightings like these had become so commonplace that she barely paid attention anymore. She learned to duck and weave to avoid confrontation. Human degradation was everywhere, and the only reasonable response seemed to be to work around it.

She entered the lobby of the office building, and the noise and chaos from the street receded into the background. Mira went to the twenty-eighth floor and paused at the front desk to check in. The view from the floor to ceiling windows was north-facing, overlooking Central Park, and extended for miles. It was an overwhelming sight. The city looked majestic and serene from this perspective, with the October sun highlighting the bursts of color across the fall treetops. Mira stopped for a moment to take in the sweeping vista. She never felt majesty or peace down on the streets of New York City anymore, but from this vantage point, she could eliminate from view all the urban rot, the garbage in the streets, and the traffic. All she saw was beauty and order. Her shoulders dropped an inch and relaxed.

Just then, her phone vibrated, and her mother's name lit up on the screen. Mira had accustomed herself to picking up her calls whenever they came in, no matter what. She held her breath in dreadful anticipation for a moment every time she said "hello," wondering if her mother was calling to say her father had died. It was a terrible thought and one she hated having, but she couldn't wish it away. One day, her mother *would* deliver that news. She steeled herself, then walked off to the side of the foyer and answered, "Hello?"

"Mira!" her mother's voice was breaking. Mira wasn't sure at first, but she thought it could be the sound of uncontrolled crying that she was hearing. She had never seen or heard her mother cry, so she didn't have a reference point for the sound. "Mira! Your...father..." Dana paused.

She was crying. Weeping, in fact. Dana could hardly speak.

Mira felt her knees weaken. The sounds of the bustling office retreated, and she couldn't hear or see anything around her. Then the office was gone, and Manhattan was gone. All that was left was Mira, curled up inside herself, bracing against an enormous wind.

"Mom!" she said firmly and a little too loudly. "Mom! Dad... what? He...what?" she demanded. Her skin felt cold, like a diabetic having a low-blood sugar episode. What good was all that mental preparation she did in anticipation of exactly this moment? She wasn't prepared—she was falling apart. Calm? Composed? Nope. Useless. She was just useless. That half-second of anticipation felt like an eternity and she was teetering on the edge of panic.

"Your father...just fired Gloria," Dana finally said, still unable to speak clearly.

Mira wobbled a bit on her feet and the sounds slowly started to return around her. She took a moment to confirm with herself that she had heard the sentence correctly and that it didn't contain the words "passed away" or "died." Her blood began to circulate again, and she straightened her legs, steadying herself. She could focus now, and she could see the meeting was about to start behind the glass wall. Her friend was motioning to her to join. She hadn't realized she had been holding her breath until she exhaled.

"Mom, my God! I thought…"

Mira was about to berate her mother for the fright but stopped herself. What she was hearing on the other end of the line was enough fear already. Adding her own to the pile seemed counterproductive.

Now that her ears were functioning again, she tried to digest what her mother had just said. "Wait, what? He fired her?" she asked. "But I just spoke to her a couple of hours ago. Didn't she just start this morning? What are you saying?"

"I don't even know what happened! I went to lie down for five minutes. He was doing some hand exercises in the next room. I could hear him getting frustrated, and then it was too quiet," Dana now said, recovering herself but still speaking quickly. "I heard the door shut and by the time I came out to see what was happening, she was gone. I can't do this alone! He can't put his socks on by himself. He can't get out of bed or wash himself yet. He had no right to let Gloria go. He didn't even give her a chance. She wasn't even here for a full day. I can't do this! He doesn't get to be a stubborn fool now, not now!"

She was right. He was being stubborn and proud, and her mother would pay a price for it that she couldn't afford to pay. But the tears? The hysterical outburst—that was the real shock.

Mira had to take a moment to absorb the wave of emotion her mother just unleashed on her. Normally, she would have been annoyed by such a dramatic display, but she could feel her mother's incredible fear and she was sympathetic. She didn't know what surprised her more—that her mother could feel such terror or that she would share what she felt with her daughter. It was a dynamic shift between them, and Mira had to readjust.

"Mom, don't worry," she said, now calm and composed. "I will be done with my board meeting in ninety minutes, and I will sort this out. It will be fixed tomorrow. Just don't worry, I am going to take care of it, okay?" She spoke as though she were the parent. It worked.

"Okay," Dana replied, her usual tone having returned. Mira could hear the embarrassment in her mother's voice immediately when she said just that one word. She had to readjust as well.

"I will come over after my meeting and help you too," Mira added. "I will get his socks on. Just don't worry."

"Okay," she repeated, this time perhaps to herself. "Thanks. Thanks, Mira," she said hurriedly. Then she hung up. She always hung up the phone abruptly, never waiting for the person on the other end of the line to say "goodbye." It was one of her quirks, and Mira knew not to read anything into it.

She walked into the boardroom and sat down next to her friend, Jeff, with whom she had served on the foundation's board for more than a decade.

"Are you okay?" he asked, seeing the look on her face.

Mira placed her phone on the table in front of her. Her mother still might call at any minute to say her father had died. "Oh, I don't even know," she said with a small chuckle. "I think I am. But every time I think that, my mother calls."

Jeff laughed. "I know what you mean. My father died two years ago, and my mother still lives in their home in New Rochelle. She can't navigate the stairs very well anymore and she insists on doing all the housework herself. I pleaded with her to sell the house and move to an apartment in the city near me. She refused. She is insulted at the suggestion that she can't manage on her own just because she is eighty-three years old. What am I going to do with that? Actually, when I think about it, she has probably made it to eighty-three because she is so stubborn."

Mira nodded in recognition of the type.

"She called me this morning and I heard a rattling sound in the background," Jeff continued, half-exasperated, half-amused. "When I asked her what the noise was, she said she was getting the stepladder out so she could change the lightbulb over the breakfast table. So, I am headed straight over there after this meeting."

Mira laughed. "It is just all so ridiculous," she said. "Maybe we should both learn not to answer our phones so often."

"Right." He lifted his notepad to reveal his phone underneath. "We probably should. But we aren't going to."

~ ~ ~

It was Dana who opened the door when Mira got to her parents' apartment that evening. Her mother was in her bathrobe and her hair was uncombed. She stared at her daughter blankly, like someone who just got off the battlefield and hadn't yet absorbed what she had just been through. It was only day one and already her mother looked defeated. Mira had no idea how she was going to do it, but she was getting Gloria back. She didn't need another parent ending up in the hospital.

Her father was lying in bed. His hands were working just enough now for him to push himself inch by inch up into a semi-seated position. Mira grabbed an extra pillow and propped it up behind him to help. She stood at the side of the bed with her arms crossed.

"What a difference a day makes!" she said, noticing his working fingers, and beginning on a positive note.

"Impressive, right?" he said sarcastically.

"Well, it's a start. But I see you aren't dexterous enough to put your hearing aid in."

She grabbed the hearing aid from its charging station on the nightstand and gently placed it in her father's ear. She then resumed her posture and glared directly at him.

"Testing, testing. Earth to Matthew Frank."

"I hear you, I hear you."

"Good. Then hear this. You need an aide. If anyone ever needed an aide, it is you. I am going to go over there tomorrow and beg that woman to come back here. And if you fire her again," she pointed to the wheelchair folded in the corner of the room, "Mom and I are going to strap you to that thing and leave you in the lobby with a sign tied around your neck that says, "Stubborn Old Man on Sale: 50% Off.""

"Is that any way to treat a patient?" he protested.

"I am not kidding, Dad. No joke. I am not about to field ten calls a day from Mom, and no one in this family is strong enough physically or mentally to bathe you daily. Your choice: Gloria or public humiliation in the lobby."

Her father looked like he was trying to come up with a retort, but he couldn't. For once in his life, he conceded, "Gloria."

~ ~ ~

Mira went to visit Gloria in Port Chester the next morning. The two women sat in the living room and Mira began to plead her case. "He won't do it again, I promise. He just can't submit to his disabilities. His instinct is to fight them, even when it is a losing battle. Once you get over how frustrating it can be, you come to see it as admirable in its own way."

Gloria smiled kindly. "Oh, that man is impossible. But don't worry, I have met plenty of men like your father before. I understand, and I haven't called the agency yet so I can come back. I do think it is admirable."

Mira let out a sigh of relief. "Really, you don't know how grateful I am—how grateful we all are. Thank you. I didn't know what I was going to do if you said no. Just please do me a favor and start off slowly with him. If he feels you are fussing over him all the time, we may end up back here again."

Gloria laughed. "I thought you said you promised it wouldn't happen again."

"You may have only spent a few hours around my father, but do you honestly think I could really make a promise like that? I was desperate."

"I will go this afternoon and get him settled for the night. Mira, don't worry."

She wished she could follow that instruction.

~ ~ ~

That evening, Mira went to her parents' apartment. Her mother passed her in the hallway and winked at her daughter as she hurried toward the door. "Headed to the supermarket." She was fully dressed and there was life in her step.

Mira turned to Gloria and winked. "A few hours of your being here worked wonders," she said, relieved.

She found her father in the kitchen drinking a cup of decaffeinated tea with great difficulty. Mostly, he was just holding the cup on the table and letting the aroma waft up to his nose. She flopped down in the chair across from him and he looked up at her over the rim of his steamed-up glasses.

"Ah, I see you are among the hearing this evening," she said, pointing to the hearing aid in his ear.

"Well, when you have a stranger escorting your naked body into the shower, you want to hear everything that is said, believe me," he explained.

"If she were thirty-five and blonde you wouldn't be complaining."

"Yeah, well, you couldn't find one of those?" Matt lowered his head a bit. "It is really humbling."

Mira was heartbroken for her father at that moment. "Dad, it isn't permanent. Look at how much movement you already have back in your hands. In a couple of weeks, this will be a funny story you embellish at the dinner table." She was forcing sunny optimism, and hoped it sounded sincere.

For the second time in two days, her father had no reply.

THERE ARE NO MAGIC CHAIRS

GLORIA ANSWERED THE DOOR WHEN Mira arrived the next day. "Come on in!" she said. "Join the party!"

Mira smiled when she saw her.

"Mr. Frank is in the living room." It was as though the last forty-eight hours never happened. They walked together to see him. Matt was sitting in "his" chair, which had been moved from the bedroom to the end of the living room near the window. It was a blue fabric recliner with wooden block arms and legs. It was more than old-fashioned; it was an artifact. It had belonged to his father and was in terrible shape, worn and tired-looking from decades of use. Matt would never allow Dana to change it. He said it contoured his body in a way no expensive, new chair ever could. It had history, and scars, like he did.

As his daughter walked in the room, he looked up and greeted her with a smile.

"Back in the saddle again," he said.

"Like you never left." She walked toward the couch across from him.

"You know, my father used to sit in this chair in our living room on West Seventy-Seventh Street, when I was a kid. He would listen to his operas on his old record player. He looked so old to me, and he was only in his early sixties. My last memory of him before he died was of him in this chair, Puccini's *La Bohème* playing in the background." He rubbed the wooden arms affectionately.

Mira and her father used to go to the opera together once upon a time too, she remembered. "That chair is seriously old. It must make you feel like a spring chicken when you sit in it!"

"It's not a magic chair, Mira," he answered. Matt shuffled a little in discomfort. Sitting too long in one position was excruciating for his broken body and even more so for his overactive mind, which was trapped in it. Even the things that gave him pleasure caused him pain.

He had several folding tables around him with assorted papers piled up on one, a cup of mint tea with lemon and three prescription bottles on another, and what looked like two small therapy balls and a pen and paper on the third.

Gloria went toward the window with a duster she didn't seem to be using and moved about quietly, turning every few minutes to pick up something Matt had knocked off one of his tables, just because she happened to be right there and why not. While she was there already, maybe she would just help him open a few pieces of mail, just because she was standing right there anyway, and why not be helpful? She would do the same for anyone sitting there even if they had full mobility in their arms.

"Can I ask why you don't do this at your desk?" Mira asked as she leaned back into the couch and grabbed a cushion, placing it on her lap. She hadn't even finished the question before she spotted his walker, his therapy equipment, the compression apparatus for his legs, and all the other paraphernalia he was using post-surgery. She realized it was hard for him to navigate the small space around the desk with everything he now needed, so he set up shop in the living room where floor space was ample. "Well," she started before her father answered, "this is a better view."

Out the window, she could see the changing leaves in Central Park and the sidewalk with people rushing up and down the streets with their children and their dogs. Matt had insisted on buying an apartment on the second floor, claiming that if ever there was a fire in the building and he had to get out via the stairs, he would at least have a shot at survival, having to navigate just the one flight down. Most New Yorkers considered second floor apartments less desirable, but for some, they offered invaluable amenities. In addition to its life-saving properties for the physically challenged, the apartment's proximity to the ground made for daily window theater. For someone who couldn't walk the streets much anymore, accessibility to the movement of the city via this view was the next best thing.

"Welcome to my world!" Matt said brightly, trying to sweep his arm left to right to feature the spread of tiny tables in front of him like a game show hostess. He didn't get very far. Mira averted her eyes. She wasn't sure if it was for her own benefit or her father's.

"How are you?" she asked him, really wanting to know the answer.

He looked up over the rim of his reading glasses at her and grinned. "I am as good as I look."

"Uh-oh. You always warned me that when someone over the age of seventy says that, there is cause for concern."

He winked at her. "How is Aaron?" he asked, inquiring about his son-in-law, but not waiting for her answer. "Be nice to that husband of yours. He is a good man. He has called every day to check in."

"I am always nice to him…when he deserves it!"

Matt paused. "I won't always be here to take care of you," he said, partly to her and partly to himself. "You are in good hands with Aaron."

Mira laughed. "Dad, are you auditioning for a role in a Jane Austen novel? Seriously."

"Oh, I miss the nineteenth century," he said wistfully and with a chuckle.

Then he changed the subject. "Daniel is coming to New York."

It was rare for her brother to return home, and she wondered why he had decided to come now. It didn't cross her mind that he would come to help his father, though maybe it should have.

Perhaps she was being unfair. Daniel wasn't a bad person, just not a particularly good son. She tried not to judge, never having been anyone's son herself, but it was hard to remain neutral about family. She had had this conversation too many times already with her parents about Daniel not coming home for the holidays, for the surgery, or for much of anything. But it only made her parents feel worse about a reality they already recognized and couldn't change. And worse, she thought, it made them feel she was complaining about being the one there with them. So, instead of saying what she was thinking, she simply said, "That's great. I'm sure he wants to make sure you are okay."

Matt seemed to be reading his daughter's mind. "Yes, I'm sure of it too."

Gloria had been dusting the bookshelf for the third time when she looked over at Matt and seemed unable to resist the impulse to tend to him any longer. "Here, let me get that." she said suddenly, as she knelt to tie his loosened shoelace. "Why are men so careless?" She made a point to include him in the larger category of hopeless men who can't take care of themselves, rather than the smaller category of those who are re-learning how to use their fingers. She was a good woman. She didn't limit her professional care to just the body.

Matt looked down at her and said, "I love it when women genuflect in front of me. It makes me feel like the king I never was!"

Gloria pulled the laces a little tighter than she needed to and ignored him entirely. Mira laughed. That was new material she hadn't heard before.

Dana walked in and smiled at Gloria. She didn't smile at too many people. She stood near Matt's impromptu desk. She was in a better-than-expected mood—she was almost cheerful, which wasn't the word often used to describe her. Mira wondered why it made her slightly uncomfortable to see her mother this way.

"I heard you speaking about Daniel's visit," Dana said.

Ah, Mira thought, *mystery solved*. At first, she had attributed her mother's good mood to Gloria's presence, and that was certainly a factor. But the real source was her son. Just the mention of Daniel made her happy. Mira was a bit envious. She used to love being around her brother herself but hadn't felt that way in years. She felt anxious before seeing him and tried to avoid him most of the time.

"He's coming on Thursday," Dana continued. "Friday night dinner will be here." She paused to allow for a possible declaration of conflicting plans that night, but when none came, she began to talk about the meal and all her children's favorite foods that she would have ready.

As she spoke, she leaned over and casually placed Matt's jar of hand wipes on the farthest part of one of his little folding tables, just at the edge of his easy grasp. She had noticed his blackened fingertips.

Matt read his newspapers the old-fashioned way, unable to navigate the tiny type on his phone and resistant to the idea of an app that could deliver the news in the same way as an actual print paper always had. The black ink that covered his fingertips once he finished scouring the pages of the *Wall Street Journal* and The Financial Times bothered him, and he always remarked that he didn't remember ink being so "cheap" when he was young. But he couldn't imagine a world without that particular annoyance in it. So, he stocked up on hand wipes, and stuck to his old ways.

He began reaching with great effort for the box Dana had placed where she knew he would have to exert some effort to get it. Mira's muscles tightened as she watched him struggle; her mother went on talking about brisket. Mira was about to get up to help her father when her mother suddenly looked at her, directly in the eyes, and asked if she wanted to bring dessert. The tone of her voice arrested Mira in place. She was being instructed to let her father help himself.

He never reached his goal, so Dana finally slid the box gently toward him, just enough so he could still claim a small victory. She never stopped talking about the dinner as she did.

Before leaving, Mira went into the kitchen to find Gloria cleaning up. She grabbed a rag and started wiping down the island countertop.

"Thank you for taking such good care of my father. You don't know what it means to me," she said, still working her way around the island.

Gloria smiled sweetly. She put down the dish she was drying and turned to Mira. "I think I do. It's hard to see them this way."

"Were you always a caregiver?" she asked, pausing as well.

Gloria seemed to stand an inch taller as she answered. "No. I was a housewife for thirty-four years. I had never worked outside the home."

Mira was surprised.

"When my husband was first diagnosed, it was mild the Parkinson's," she continued. She added "the" as though the disease were a character in the book of her life, like the Devil. "I could do everything, and I did. I wouldn't let anyone else near him. He was the love of my life, and I was going to do it all. When it got a little worse, I helped him into the shower, and cut his food. And when it got worse than that I got him dressed, and up and down the stairs."

She paused and shook her head.

"Then one day, he fell in the walk-in closet, and I couldn't lift him up. He lay there for half an hour until the ambulance came. I cried the entire time watching him there on the floor, humiliated and helpless. And for two days after that I couldn't stop crying. Then, finally, I hired an aide. Viktor was wonderful all those months. I couldn't have done it without him. When Martin died, I promised myself I would help others." She spoke proudly.

Mira silently marveled at the number of times she felt surprised by people and their stories. No matter how often she discovered unexpected strength, or nobility, or courage in others, it always stopped her in her tracks.

She put down the rag and looked at her directly. "Well, you are absolutely helping my father. And we are all grateful to you," she said with great emotion.

Gloria gently answered, "You are so welcome, dear." Then she looked at Mira with a smirk and said, "You know, he is a real piece of work, your father."

"Yes, I am aware," she answered.

"That will work to his advantage. He doesn't go down easily. If I don't end up strangling him, he will get through this and be around for a long time."

"Yes, well that's a big if," Mira joked. She leaned back against the counter and folded her arms across her chest. "You know, I used to think that 'a long time' meant decades. Now, I hope… well, I still hope it means that, but of course…" She let her unfinished thought trail off.

"Yes, I understand," Gloria responded right away, so Mira wouldn't have to finish.

She reached out and touched her arm warmly. "I know you do."

~ ~ ~

When Mira arrived home, she called out for Aaron to see if he was there.

"In the office," he replied.

He often was. She walked in and sighed at the sight of stacks of papers strewn across the desk. Aaron always insisted he had a system and the thousands of pages surrounding him weren't what they appeared to be—a disorganized mess. He turned around and smiled at her, raising his finger to his lips to signal that he needed silence. He was on a business call. She walked quietly to the couch next to his desk and sat, watching him as he worked.

He was handsome, she thought. Aaron had thick, dark hair, the kind men half his age dreamt of. He was tall and his shoulders still looked like those of a former athlete who rowed for his university team. He was wearing his usual khaki pants slightly too big at the waist, old black loafers and a blue plaid button-down shirt that he kept open at the collar. He always looked refined and expensive, but he was never fashionable. Looking like he spent more than twenty minutes on himself didn't suit him, he used to say. Mira didn't try to upgrade his outfits anymore. His look was familiar, and she thought she might miss it if he suddenly changed it.

Aaron hung up the phone and came over to the couch to sit beside his wife. He kissed her on the forehead as he settled next to her. "How is your dad?" he asked, as he always did.

"He is moving his arms a little more, I guess," she said softly.

"Good," he answered optimistically. There was no other way he could answer—he was always optimistic about everything.

"How is work? All good?" Mira asked, leaning against his shoulder. She didn't have the energy to get more specific. She just wanted a thumbs up or a thumbs down so she would know whether there was anything to worry about.

"All good," he replied reassuringly. It was quiet for a moment and then Aaron asked his next question, with equal optimism. "Did you speak to your parents about Florida?"

She didn't know how he could possibly ask with any hope that she had spoken to them, given that he had asked that same question dozens of times over the last year and never got an answer in the affirmative. But he was very clever, she thought, never to turn this conversation into a confrontation. Mira shuddered at the thought of disappointing him. It wasn't any easier now that she had so much practice at it.

"I couldn't," she said apologetically, her head still on his shoulder.

They had never formally made the decision to move but were considering it very seriously for a while. Mira had intended to raise the possibility with her parents and see what their reaction might be. She never did. Then, her father learned he would need the second surgery, and she stopped even trying to work up the courage to talk about it with them. It was unspoken, but understood, between Aaron and Mira that there was little momentum left in the idea, but it still came up once in a while. Aaron mostly asked to get Mira to confirm out loud what he already knew. But she wasn't ready yet to close the door on something she knew her husband wanted.

She didn't need to say any more. He pulled her in and gave her a reassuring hug. "Maybe next time, my girl."

~ ~ ~

Mira was at the salon. She looked straight into the mirror and greeted Nick who approached from behind and put his hands directly into her hair, tousling it a bit and inspecting it back through the reflection in the mirror like a stylist prepping a model for a photoshoot.

Nick had been her hairdresser for ten years. They knew each other as well as Mira knew most of her city friends whom she saw three times a year for dinner. She knew about his last boyfriend who left him six years ago after he had his first knee surgery and subsequently gained thirty pounds. She knew about his Catholic upbringing and his interest in investing. She loved his "old days" stories about epic parties in Ibiza when he was "young and hot" and his current stories about his socialite clients who teetered in on their heels and spilled about their husbands and their boyfriends.

He would whisper tales of tipsy middle-aged women stumbling across the reception area at two o'clock in the afternoon after their long lunches of white wine and lettuce leaves. Blurry-eyed and unsteady on their feet, they often didn't notice the glass divider just off the elevator with the salon name etched onto it. They would bang their foreheads and wobble toward the front desk giggling at themselves. The cleaning woman kept a bottle of Windex and a rag handy to wipe away the smears of makeup the ladies left behind.

Nick loved the assortment of crazy, straight, wealthy women who sat in his chair. He loved their secrets and their flaws. Mira loved hearing about them as much as he loved talking about them. Once he was done gossiping, they would talk about politics and podcasts, and she loved that about him even more.

"So!" he exclaimed. "What are we doing today, my lovely?"

Mira opened her mouth to answer, but before the words came out, she stopped and noticed his beard. The last time she had seen him, he said he was going to shave it off before going home to see his mother in Pennsylvania in a month's time. The beard was still there.

"Wait," she started, "did you already see your mother and keep the beard or…" she trailed off, pausing to do the calculation in her head. "Was I just here three weeks ago?"

Ding, ding, ding. She could actually hear the realization bell go off in her own head. She was, in fact, last at the salon three weeks earlier to get her hair colored, and she needed another treatment already. Her roots were wiry and gray, and they were very visible against her dark brown hair. "Oh my God," she said aloud, still taking it in.

"It's one of the gifts of age, baby," Nick said laughing a little, clearly having had this conversation with others.

"But I used to color my hair maybe twice a year at most," she insisted, protesting to no one in particular.

Nick's hands were reassuring on her shoulders. He leaned down and put his face next to hers, looking at her through the mirror. "You were in your thirties and early forties then," he explained. "Everything after forty-five is a race to maintain yourself so you don't scare young children in the street," he joked. "The more mileage in the car, the more often you have to bring it in for repair."

Mira frowned. "You're not allowed to compare me to an old car," she retorted. "You are supposed to make me feel pretty!"

"Ha!" Nick bellowed with a clap of his hands. "Oh, my love, I can make you *look* pretty, I promise you that. But you are in charge of making yourself *feel* pretty."

"Words of wisdom from the gay man with the tattoo of a naked woman on his triceps," she said with approval. "I guess I'll take wisdom wherever I can get it."

Nick winked at her and got to work. Mira heard herself speaking and thought suddenly that she sounded so much like her father.

IF EVERYONE GOT
WHAT THEY DESERVED...

THE NEXT MORNING, SHE WOKE up early and ordered an Uber to take her to Brooklyn. Mira had been visiting Mae once every two weeks for years, bringing food and whatever else she thought she might need. Mae was living with her grandnephew, Willie, who was unemployed and occupying the larger of the two bedrooms in the tiny apartment. He had convinced his elderly great-aunt to move into the smaller room and Mira added that offense to the list of things she never forgave him for. Matt had been paying the rent and all the bills. He had repeatedly begged Mae to come and live with him and Dana, but she wouldn't leave her home.

The drive down the FDR was slow. It was raining lightly and everything in New York City stalled at even the slightest hint of precipitation. The wet buildings and dark skies made Manhattan seem even drearier than it was. As they made their way south, the scenery struck Mira as gloomy, and she wondered how so many people could overlook the objective ugliness of New York and choose to live there. She wondered how she herself had done it.

She arrived at the building on the corner of Bergen Street, just a few blocks in from Atlantic Avenue. It was a four-story, box-like structure with small windows and a simple gray façade. Mae had lived there for decades, choosing it because it was around the corner from her church. Mira had never been there but always wished she had. There was a limit to how well she could know Mae without knowing her church, she thought.

The apartment was three flights up. The stairs were dark metal, rusty, and steep. Mira was carrying bags for Mae, and by the second floor, her leg muscles were burning. It was always entirely quiet inside the building, as though everything stopped when she walked in. She had never, in all the years she had been coming, seen anyone in the halls or the stairwell or picked up the sound of a television through the doors. It felt like such a sad and lonely place to grow old.

Willie opened the door. He wasn't much taller than Mira at five foot six and he always wore a black woolen cap, which he removed and lifted an inch into the air when he greeted Mira, like a chauffeur in an old movie. She never understood why he did that.

"How are you today, Miss Mira?" he cheerfully asked, as he always did. Their interaction was scripted by now.

"Fine, thanks, Willie, and you?" she replied while moving past him and bringing her bags over to the table.

"I can help you with those," he offered.

"No thanks, Willie," she answered, practically cutting him off with her back turned to him. "I may look small, but I am pretty strong."

She could feel him hesitating, trying to think of what to say next and how to hang around to see what groceries she had brought, but he didn't come up with anything.

"Well, I have to go," he said before heading out the door. And that was everything he had ever really said to Mira in all the years they had known each other.

Mira didn't like him. She had never arrived to find Mae sitting at the table with her nephew chatting or seen a cup of tea placed next to her bed. To him, Mae was a source of rent and food and nothing more.

She began to unpack, pulling a block of sharp cheddar out of the bag and grumbling to herself as she loaded it into the refrigerator. She had a skirt steak, twelve cans of root beer, a jar of chili flakes, and a chocolate-frosted Entenmann's cake with her. Half of her grocery list was for Willie, not Mae.

As she slammed each item down on the table, she called her father to complain.

"Willie doesn't deserve this," she said, seething with resentment.

"Mira, if the world gave everyone what they deserved, we would all be in trouble," he answered. She wasn't satisfied.

"Think of this as a gift for Mae, not Willie," he added. "The goal is to make her life easier and better. If he is content, then our goal is easier to achieve."

Her father had long ago made his peace with Willie, but Mira couldn't.

"He could do more, and he doesn't."

"Mira, are you sure you know what he is capable of? What he can and can't do?" Matt challenged her. "Do what *you* are capable of and stop worrying about others."

"Why do you have to be so reasonable when I am trying to vent emotionally?" she replied, acknowledging his point, but resisting it.

"Send my love to Mae," he said, chuckling.

They hung up. Mira knew her father was right, but she still resented Willie for not loving Mae the way she thought he should.

She unpacked a family size bag of salt and vinegar potato chips and felt triggered. She knew it was childish when she picked up the soda cans and shook them, but she enjoyed the thought of Willie opening them later.

The apartment was small and clean. The living room, dining room, and kitchen were all in one space. There was a small rectangular table with two metal chairs pushed up against the wall under a window, and a two-seat, low, gray sofa with a wooden side table on one side and a floor lamp on the other against a long, bare wall. The kitchen was more of a kitchenette lining the opposite wall of the room, with a white refrigerator, white cabinets, and a builders' grade beige stone countertop. There was one green potted plant on the windowsill and a small colorful mat on the floor near the sink.

Mira walked around the corner into Mae's tiny room. Her twin bed, a small nightstand with her Bible and reading glasses on it, a chest of four drawers and a large color television the Franks had bought her to watch her baseball games on, filled the room entirely. Mae lay under three layers of bedding and her hair was wrapped as it always was. A few straggling strands of gray peeked out, and her almost entirely white eyebrows stood in stark contrast to her dark skin. Her formerly full frame had shrunk over time and her cheeks were almost hollow.

Mira had only ever viewed Mae as an older woman. She looked ancient now, beyond age. Mira felt she was in the presence of someone half on this earth and half in the next. The transition her body was making became more and more evident each time she visited. It was reducing in on itself, ridding itself of every unnecessary cell. She looked so small. Mae's dark eyes tilted to the right and brought her head along with them as she turned to look at Mira.

"Mira, baby, is that you?"

"It's me!" she said loudly so Mae could hear her voice.

"Lord, I thank you! Thank you for bringing my Mira to me."

"You look surprised to see me! Were you expecting your boyfriend?"

"Girl, I aint stuttin' bout you!" she said, laughing. Mae was always a little surprised to see Mira even though she could have set her watch to her visits. The surprise, Mira thought, really was immense gratitude. Mae never expected anything from anyone. When she did receive something, from a visit to a gift on her birthday, she thanked God. Mira felt grateful too.

"Mae, let's get you up and to the table," she said, reaching over to help her out of bed. Mae smelled like the jars of Noxzema cream she used to cover herself in years ago. The scent took Mira back to the days when everything seemed constant and unchangeable. She breathed it in deeply, carefully walking Mae to the kitchen table and making her some tea and toast with her favorite jam.

Then she got busy removing all the bedding and replacing it with fresh linens. She cleaned the small room with a special lavender-scented cleanser Mae once remarked reminded her of a perfume she got for her first anniversary from her late husband. Matt had been paying a cleaning woman to come to the apartment twice a week, but Mira liked helping keep Mae's home tidy as well. Tending to her felt like just reimbursement.

When she finished, she took Mae by the arm and walked her in circles around the room, to get her circulation going. They walked slowly, and as they did, Mae started to hum a tune that sounded like an old spiritual. She didn't have a particularly great voice, and it was broken up by age, but Mira found it soothing. There was still energy in her old body, enough to conjure up a song.

Mira brought her back to bed to rest and dragged one of the kitchen table chairs into the room and sat by her as she slept. *What was this life?* she thought, looking at the body there in the bed.

Mae had gotten such joy from scanning the letters in her tattered old Bible, delicately moving her finger across the page to ensure she saw every word. Now, her eyes had deteriorated, and she could do no more than hold her precious book and almost inaudibly speak passages she remembered by heart from church. The oversized television on the wall made the Mets games watchable, but Mira could often see Mae squinting as she tried to make out who was at bat. She didn't have a long or aspirational list of joys in life, and the two she did have were taken away. It seemed cruel.

Though Mae likely never filed a complaint with God for allowing her last years on earth to be this way, Mira had issued a few on her behalf. It was a long, lonely slide and it seemed an unjust reward for a life spent in complete faithfulness, honesty, and kindness. Then she thought about her father's warning not to expect that people get what they "deserved."

She pulled out her phone and started checking her emails. Jeff had forwarded a link to a lecture by a rabbi whose weekly online class he attended. The subject line read, "This helped me a lot".

Mira clicked on it and a video popped up. The rabbi was a young, clean-shaven man who spoke passionately about the imperative to acknowledge life's sanctity, even as its quality diminished. He was animated as he spoke, pacing back and forth in front of his audience and gesticulating with his arms. Mira appreciated the thought, but she wondered if he would be as enthusiastic about it if he were unable to wave his hands around or confined to his bed. It felt like a soothing sentiment for the caregiver, but cold comfort for the one receiving the care.

Mae suddenly opened her eyes. "Mira, you here?" she asked, again surprised.

"Well, I hope so. If I am not, you are talking to yourself."

Mae laughed. "I ain't stuttin' 'bout you, girl," she said. "How are Daddy's hands?" Matt's health was always the first thing on her mind.

"He is getting stronger every day." Technically, it was true. He did have more movement than immediately after the surgery, but that wasn't saying much. Mira was worried. She had long ago learned not to expect miracles when it came to her father's health but, foolishly, she had convinced herself that his condition couldn't get any worse. And then it did. She now lived with the humbling and terrifying awareness that everything could always get worse. What if he couldn't recover functional use of his hands? What would happen then? She tried again to think about "sanctity."

"The Lord will touch his body, Mira," Mae said, channeling a message from somewhere, something. She looked unshakable as she said it, and her voice was as strong as it had ever been. She meant it, whether it was God himself talking through her, or the deepest part of her soul willing it to be God's will too. "You have to praise Him," she said. Mira was holding her hand now, trying to feel the energy in Mae's own broken-down body as she prayed over someone else's. It was a prayer, she thought, and prayer has power. Or she truly hoped it did.

She felt a flash of shame, clinging to a cold, fleshless old woman's hand looking for strength. It was preposterous, she thought. She was there to help Mae. "If you say it, I will believe it," Mira said softly.

Mae began to lean forward and struggled to her elbows. Mira helped her sit up and propped extra pillows behind her. She recognized the look on her face. She had seen it hundreds of times before. The spirit that inhabited her was urgent and animating. Her voice strengthened and her gaze was more focused. Her cheeks seemed to expand and increase in volume. "The Lord is going to touch Matthew," she exclaimed again, releasing what was passing through her, like a preacher from the pulpit in transmission of an inspired message. "He will touch him," she persisted, almost involuntarily. She was like a vessel being filled up and pouring its contents out on command. "What He has said has already been done."

Mira closed her eyes and breathed in deeply. She didn't believe or disbelieve Mae's messages. She clung to them. They were the words of someone who loved her and her father and her family unconditionally. Who cared if that someone was God Himself or Miss Mae Boyd?

Mae started coughing and trying to clear her throat, struggling to talk. Mira brought another cup of tea back to her bedside. She gently spooned the warm liquid into Mae's mouth, careful not to spill anything on her night dress.

"And how is Mommy?" Mae then asked. Mira was caught off guard. They didn't talk about her mother that much. "I think… fine," she stumbled, "I mean she is fine." Mae seemed to be considering something for a moment and then she said, "She has her art. I am glad she do. She needs that, you know." Mira didn't know exactly what that meant, but she nodded in agreement.

"When you are ready, we have to get you up and out of that bed again," Mira said, changing the subject. "You have to make your famous brisket for when Daniel gets home." The brisket was legendary, and it wasn't Daniel's favorite. It was hers. She knew Mae would never stand over the stove and cook it for her again, but she loved the thought of it.

"Girl, I ain't makin' no brisket, no way, no how," Mae laughed. She knew too, but the memory of the Frank family stove and the incredible meals she made there brought a smile to her face.

"Want me to read to you?" Mira asked, knowing the answer. She picked up the Bible. She loved the feel of the cheap, fake-leather cover, and swept over the surface of it with her hand. Flakes of the edges had long ago fallen off, revealing the brown cardboard underlay. The oils from Mae's hands had discolored every page, many of which were yellowed with age. She could smell the Noxzema wafting up from the decaying old book and the sensory trigger was a gift.

She opened to a random page as she always did, and landed in the Book of Jeremiah, chapter 2, verse 2: "Thus saith the LORD; I remember thee, the kindness of thy youth, the love of thine espousals, when thou wentest after me in the wilderness, in a land that was not sown." Mira spoke each word slowly and with meaning, and Mae breathed in deeply as she spoke. She couldn't fully understand why, but she knew Mae felt remembered by her God there in that tiny, bare room to which she was mostly confined. He was with her even as she slowly wasted away. Jeremiah was speaking words of comfort to a nation that had turned its back on God. If He could remember and love them, then what awaited a devotee like Mae? Mira was comforted by the thought a little.

"Mae, what was Dad like when he was young?" she asked after closing the Bible.

Mae looked surprised by the question, but she answered right away. These days, she was able to recall details about her life from decades ago more easily than from last week. "Oh, Matthew was such a good boy!" she said, lighting up as her mind seemed to be playing back a video in her head from seventy years ago.

"He used to run around after that dog of his, tryin' to catch its tail. That dog didn't like that none," she remembered, starting to laugh.

Mira closed her eyes and tried to imagine a little boy with her father's face on it running, but she couldn't.

"Do you know that every week when I did the washin' down in the basement, he would come and help me? He could hardly carry nothin' but he never would let me do all that heavy liftin' on my own," Mae said as if she were sharing the most important information about him. "Oh, he was a good boy, your daddy." She smiled at the thought of it.

Mira smiled too. "He told me about the laundry in the basement, but he didn't mention he tried to help." She wished she had a memory of her father lifting something heavy. She was happy to have one of Mae's. "Mae, can I ask you something else?" Mira had always wondered, and had never asked. "Why do you like baseball so much?"

Mae smiled at the question. "My husband, you know he knew everything 'bout baseball. He used to read so many books 'bout the numbers and this player do this and that player do that. He talked 'bout it all the time. Lord knows he talked 'bout all kind of numbers *all* the time. He was good with all that too, always was. But he could never find no work like that back then, you know. That's how it was. He told me that baseball was an American game, and he was an American, so he was gonna watch it. I never did watch it with him though." She paused for a moment and then continued. "When he died, I took Joseph with me to see a game at the big stadium there in Brooklyn and I said we was goin' to watch it too. I always did watch baseball on TV ever since."

Mira pulled back in her chair as Mae finished speaking, stunned by the story and by the realization that she had never heard it before. "I shouldn't have always changed the channel in your room on Friday nights while you were watching the game," she said softly. "I'm sorry, Mae. I didn't know."

Mae chuckled. "Girl, you was always pestering me so! But I wasn't mad. I loved havin' you come and stay in my room with me. You was my baby girl."

"Did you love your husband very much?" Mira asked.

"Child, that man was a good man. A good man."

"You know, when I was a child, I just thought you were part of *our* family. It never occurred to me…"

The front door slammed, and Mira heard Willie come into the apartment. He didn't come in to say hello or to check if his aunt needed anything. Mira poked her head out of the doorway and saw nothing, but she noticed the Entenmann's cake he loved so much was gone. She went to the kitchen to make herself some tea, and then Willie walked in.

He handed Mira a mug with a bright yellow flower painted on the front. It looked handmade. The handle had a noticeable crack in it that had been crudely repaired with glue.

"My aunt likes this cup," he said. "I thought you could use it when you make her some tea."

Mira looked at the mug and then directly at Willie. "I will make sure to use it."

He didn't say anything else. He just nodded and returned to his room. She held the mug in her hand and wondered if he had made it.

Mira lingered for another hour as Mae drifted in and out of sleep. She used the time to text Lilly and to check her emails. She watched Mae and listened to her shallow breath. She thought that if she stared directly at her for a sustained period, perhaps she would see the decline happening in real time, right in front of her. Would she see her eyes sink in a bit lower, or catch gravity pulling the skin down on her neck? The changes had been slow over time, but surely there is a moment, a split second where the shift takes place, she imagined. If she could catch that moment, maybe she could arrest it. Maybe she could understand the enemy.

But she couldn't. After a while, she grew weary and berated herself for her magical thinking. She made Mae a plate of food and placed it on the chair she had been sitting on next to the bed. She put the TV remote next to the Bible on the nightstand and left.

FAMILY DINNER

THAT FRIDAY NIGHT, MIRA ARRIVED at her parents' apartment late. She had been waiting at home for the dishwasher repair man.

"Sorry!" she called as she came through the door pulling off her jacket. "Labor shortages now mean you have to be grateful to wait in your apartment over a four-hour window, which is never honored, to get an appliance fixed. I am supposed to count myself lucky that he came at all," she said, dropping herself onto the sofa next to Aaron who had been there for half an hour visiting with his in-laws.

"Don't worry. I was just showing your husband my latest sleight of hand card trick," Matt joked.

Mira rolled her eyes. "Very funny."

Just then, Daniel popped out from around the corner with a scotch in his hand. "Hey, sis," he said, walking in. Mira and Aaron stood up together. Aaron reached out to shake his brother-in-law's hand as Mira waited and looked on.

Daniel was six foot two and lean. He and his sister looked nothing alike. His round face and light hair made for endless family jokes about some Cossack from four generations ago falling in love with a Jewish girl in the shtetl he was supposed to burn down and passing his genetic material on to Daniel. He was wearing his usual uniform of jeans and a sweatshirt. He proudly told everyone he met that he hadn't been seen in a suit since his bar mitzvah. He was in this regard, and in so many others, the opposite of his father who hadn't been seen in anything other than a suit since his.

Mira hugged Daniel in the awkward way they had grown accustomed to over the last several years. It was stiff and brief. The ghost of their once close relationship made the current discomfort more pronounced than if there had always been a distance between them. But even through the strangeness of the moment, there were lingering memories of a bond that she recalled sweetly. As children, they had played on the floor of his room for hours. He had elaborate sets of Hot Wheels racetracks and cars in every shape and color, which he carefully sorted through and ranked according to his preferences. He would squeal with excitement as he ordered his big sister to watch the cars collide and crash onto the ground. She followed all his orders, happy to oblige him in any way she could. She adored him. The sound of his laugh and the pure joy he projected were infectious, and she missed it all now.

"Hi, baby brother," she said with a smile, remembering.

Dana sat close to Daniel at dinner. Mira and Aaron sat beside Matt and the Franks' oldest friends, David and Susie Baum, who filled out the table along with Dr. Baron, an elderly widower and regular guest at the Frank dinner table. Wine was poured into silver cups at each place and the traditional challah bread was covered with the blue and silver embroidered silk cover the family had been using since Mira was a child.

It was always hard to get everyone to stop talking long enough to say the prayers before the meal, and Matt had to try several times to silence everyone before he successfully interrupted the chatter. Together, everyone sang "Sholom Aleichem," welcoming in the Sabbath angel. Everyone except Daniel.

Then Matt spoke up. "Son!" he said loudly and firmly, "will you say *kiddush* please?"

Aaron quickly interjected and volunteered for the job. "I know I only learned Hebrew two years ago," he said, turning all eyes at the table away from Daniel and toward him, "but if I don't practice, it is as good as gone. I'll do the prayer over the wine if you don't mind, Dan." Mira put her hand on his knee as both a gesture of thanks and a request not to appeal after her father would politely shoot him down, which she knew he would.

Matt jumped in before Aaron's offer could be accepted. "It's not every day I have my son here," Matt said looking directly at Daniel who was refilling his scotch glass. "Thank you, Aaron, but, son, please, go ahead."

Daniel grimaced and looked down. He reached begrudgingly for the small prayer book and fumbled for the right page. He sighed and then began to recite the blessing. He didn't stand, as was the custom. Slowly, without drawing too much attention to herself, Dana grabbed the black suede kippah still sitting on the table next to Daniel's plate and gently put it on his head as he read. He read the prayer rather than sing it in the traditional fashion, but his Hebrew was nearly perfect.

Mira was holding her small prayer book in her hands, tracing the etched gold lettering on the front with her right forefinger, the way Mae drew her fingers across the pages of her Bible. Feeling the letters that spelled out the name of her brother and the date of his bar mitzvah, which were engraved on the cover, was an exercise in trying to retrieve the feeling of that time, so many years ago. The indentations of the type tickled her fingertip and she looked away from her brother and down at her hand and smiled softly.

Aaron leaned into Mira and whispered in her ear. "Why is this so important to your dad?" She thought for a moment. "Maybe Hebrew is the only language he feels they have left in common," she quietly offered, surprising herself. Once she heard herself say it, she thought it wasn't a bad answer to the question. But she wasn't convinced it was the complete answer either.

When he was done, Dr. Baron yelled "Amen!" and made a fisted "atta-boy" gesture with his hand in Daniel's direction. Daniel raised an eyebrow, shot a half-smile at the old man, and took a sip of his drink.

Aaron sprang up from his seat and the sound of the chair dragging back against the floor interrupted the momentary awkward silence. "I am doing the challah!" he announced, pretending he wanted the job so he could show off his Hebrew skills on that blessing. But really, he was kindly relieving his father-in-law of the embarrassment of not being able to cut the bread. Mira looked at her husband with gratitude.

As the food started arriving at the table, the conversation began. Dr. Baron talked about the library he had run for fifty years at the Historical Society and its complete conversion to digital archives.

"No one comes in anymore," he said with a resigned shrug and an acceptance of the technological shift that had made his life's work seem obsolete. "Everyone just looks up what they want on the computer. What are they going to do with all those books?"

He and Matt talked often about all the things that seem to have vanished from the world that they missed. Mira loved listening to them, not for their laments, but for the love of what they were lamenting. What would she miss that much when she was around eighty? She often wondered.

"Danny," Susie Baum broke in, "tell us about Los Angeles, darling. How is everything going?" *Everything* was a deliberately generic term because no one knew what Daniel was *actually* doing in LA. For some time, Mira had been afraid to ask. She wasn't sure if she was afraid of upsetting her brother with the question, or of upsetting herself with knowledge of whatever the answer might be. He hadn't had a real full-time job for as long as she could remember. He was always "working on a project," but no one quite knew what that meant. After a few years, everyone stopped asking. The look in Daniel's eyes told them he wouldn't keep coming home for holiday dinners if he was going to get grilled about his work. Like properly trained puppies, the Franks and their close friends obeyed their silent orders.

Susie seemed to have momentarily slipped and forgotten the rules. Daniel looked at the refilled scotch glass in his hand rather than at Susie. He was about to open his mouth to say something, but Susie, realizing her mistake, cut him off before he could. Mira saw her mother holding her breath as she held her own.

"Oh, I am just so happy to see you, Danny!" Susie gushed. "Really, just having you home is so special. Have I told you about Bill at the club? You have to hear what he did!" She pivoted into a story about Daniel's old golf partner and Mira could see her brother's grip loosen on his glass, the blood returning to his relaxing fingers. He was laughing with Susie now and recalling funny stories from years ago. They were a table full of hostages.

The Baums once had a son Daniel's age. Andy Baum and Daniel Frank met in pre-school and were inseparable through the third grade. The two families grew close through their boys and spent almost every Friday night together. Then, one ordinary Sunday evening, Andy choked to death on a hard candy he had been sucking on while jumping on his bed. David and Susie found him when they came into his room to tuck him in. He hadn't made a sound or run down the hallway for help. It was a crack in the foundation of their lives, and no one in either family ever fully recovered. Susie became like a second mother to Daniel, whom she loved unconditionally. She didn't know what he was doing in Los Angeles either, Mira thought, but it didn't matter, as long as he returned. Not every son did.

Susie's shoulder-length blond hair bobbed up and down as she spoke excitedly with Daniel. Mira mused to herself that Susie's hair follicles were dancing with joy at the mere sight of him. She held her husband's hand as she spoke. Dana clearly had the same physical reaction to her son that her friend did, only more. Daniel seemed to electrify his mother. Not so his father. Matt didn't bounce witticisms and banter off his son the way he did with Mira, his hospital nurse, or the guy at the front desk at his office building. There was no live energy between father and son. It all seemed distant and flat. Even so, Matt could never take his eyes off his son when they were in the room together, as though he felt every time might be the last. Daniel rarely looked directly at his father, Mira noticed, as though the last time he did was really the last time.

Dr. Baron interrupted. "How are the girls in California, Dan?" he asked with real interest. Daniel laughed. "Great, actually. Want me to set you up with a hot thirty-year-old, Dr. Baron?" Her brother could certainly impersonate his father, Mira thought, despite his seeming dislike of him.

"What makes you think I don't have one of those right here?" Dr. Baron replied. "Some women love old men with bald heads and bad hearing. I have to fight them off with my cane!" he insisted. Then he paused and turned to Matt. "Remember when we did have to fight them off, Matt?"

"Yes, actually, I do. Clearly. I think it was the Nixon administration," Matt said jokingly.

"You're lucky," Dr. Baron answered, "I am so old I can barely remember yesterday, let alone decades ago. But I'm such a good-looking guy, I'm sure it's true. I'm sure those girls couldn't keep their hands off me."

Aaron laughed. "If you can't remember, you should just rewrite those girls as models with PhDs. Say they fought over you," he offered.

Dr. Baron nodded in approval, raising his eyebrows, and curling his lower lip in appreciation of the idea. "One of the few benefits of old age," he said, "is the license you get to tell your life story however you like. There aren't enough people alive to contradict what you say!"

Dana let out a sigh. "What a cheerful thought," she said sarcastically. Mira then noticed her mother had been cutting Matt's food on his plate while everyone's attention had been focused on Dr. Baron's senior citizen routine. At the same time, she slid his water glass a few inches away from his plate, making it just a bit harder to reach. When she was done, she brought the basket of challah bread over to Daniel. She paused next to him for a moment as he helped himself, her hand gently resting on his shoulder, like a phone charger plugging into an outlet. Her eye caught Susie's and they smiled warmly at one another.

"Okay," Dr. Baron conceded, "I will change the subject. No more old. Only young. Aaron, how is work?"

Aaron looked startled. "Am I now the definition of young?" he asked. "I am fifty-two!"

"Young is still having a barber," Dr. Baron said, rubbing his head.

Aaron smiled. "Well, then, I am young I guess," he replied. "Work is great. We're opening the Miami office just after the New Year."

Mira tensed up, but luckily, Dr. Baron couldn't think of a follow-up question.

David Baum jumped in. "Matt, we're headed to Florida at the end of November for the winter," he started. "When are you coming?"

Matt attempted to wave his hand dismissively. "I can't travel," he said flatly. "I can hardly get in and out of a chair on my own."

David was unmoved. "So, you get in a wheelchair and you just do it. Stop being so proud."

Mira wasn't sure if David was always so direct or if the loss of his only child made him impatient with anything less than a life-or-death excuse for refusing to life to its fullest. He regularly demanded his old friend join him at dinner, the theater, or anywhere else a wheelchair could reach. He was regularly turned down, but he never stopped asking.

As the two argued, David pushed his chair back from the table using just his legs and stood up to reach across his wife and grab the heavy water pitcher to her left. He raised it with one arm and poured for himself and Susie. Then he lowered himself down again into his seat. He was just one year younger than her father but in entirely different physical condition. He was strong, nimble, and steady.

Mira was envious on her father's behalf. Watching men his age play tennis or run a half marathon never bothered her. Those were the genetically blessed 1 percent, she reasoned. She didn't envy them because she knew only the lucky few inherited that lot. It was the old man simply sitting in the bleachers at the baseball game with his grandson, or the grandfather in the swimming pool with his granddaughter whom she jealously regarded. There were so many of them in the world—men who move a little slower than they used to, but who still move. Her father wasn't one of them. How great it would be just to see him reach across a table or get out of a chair without an assist.

Her thoughts were interrupted by the ongoing back and forth. "Listen, they don't need another broken-down old man in Florida, Dave," Matt deflected, trying to end the debate. He was cupping his glass of hot decaffeinated tea in his hands, soaking the heat into his fingers. "You go and eat dinner at a quarter to six and drive fifteen miles per hour under the speed limit on my behalf. I am staying here."

David shot a look at Dana who seemed to silently thank him for trying. The debate was over, and they both knew it.

"Matt, you are impossible," he said, relenting. "But, I will have you know that I have never booked a dinner reservation before six o'clock."

When dinner was over, Daniel said a quick good night and headed down the hall to the guest room. Mira had hardly spoken to him. Dana asked, again, if he had everything he needed, and if she could get him anything. If he had asked her to fluff his pillow and rub his feet, she would have been honored, Mira thought. It made her sad, but not for herself. Mira watched Daniel leave the room without making a plan to see him again before he was to return home. She hugged her father goodbye and lingered a split second longer than usual, then grabbed Aaron by the arm and left.

~ ~ ~

Saturday afternoon was unusually warm and Aaron was anchored to his desk surrounded by stacks of paper.

Mira poked her head into the office and Aaron acknowledged her without turning around. "You have built-in shelves and file drawers on either side of the desk, and they are very under-utilized," she remarked. "If you aren't going to organize your papers, maybe I can use the space for my shoes."

Aaron turned around. "Even threats of more shoe shopping won't move me. I know where everything is. I have a system."

"Right, I know," she said, smirking. "Anyway, I am not sure I would recognize you if you didn't have towers of documents surrounding you. They have become part of your look." Content, he turned back to his computer.

She leaned her head against the doorpost. "I'm going to go check in on Dad."

"Good, sure," he said quickly, completely focused on the screen in front of him. Then, suddenly, he turned around to look at her and smiled. "I have to get a lot of reading done. Say hello for me."

Mira started to leave, and Aaron called after her. She turned back around to face him. "Don't bring up the move, Mira," he said plainly, without any emotion. She stood in place and didn't say a word. She simply looked at her husband and nodded.

"I know…" he began but then stopped short of acknowledging what they both already knew.

"Nothing is final yet," Mira offered. But somehow, they both knew it was.

He closed his eyes for a moment, sighed, and then opened them again, staring straight into his wife's eyes. "If my parents were still alive, I'm not sure I could leave them either."

THE THINGS YOU NOTICE

MIRA ARRIVED AT THE FRANKS' apartment and Gloria let her in. She was already shaking her head in exasperation as the door opened, and Mira knew who had exasperated her. She sensed a big Christmas bonus in Gloria's future and knew she would earn it.

Matt was in his usual chair in the living room. When Mira entered, he was leaned over with his eyeglasses on the tip of his nose looking down into a book. She recognized what he was reading right away. He had stopped going to synagogue on Saturdays years ago. He couldn't get in and out of the pews and he refused, of course, to go in a wheelchair. He didn't miss the prayers particularly, but he loved to read the weekly Torah portion and committed to doing so on his own each week.

His Bible wasn't quite as old or tattered as Mae's, but it was getting there. The pages were thin and made a distinct crinkling sound as Matt turned them. The typeface was tiny, and Mira used to tease her father that the publisher must also be in the magnifying glass business, but he refused to buy a new book with larger print. He simply drew the old book closer and closer to his face.

She loved to watch her father studying the text. On the surface, it was the opposite experience of watching Mae scan her letters. He read every word, investigated each of the commentators, and reflected on every interpretation. It was a deeply academic pursuit. But there was an obvious spiritual absorption she could see in her father's body language as he read as well. It was the same kind of intensity and personal encounter she saw in Mae when her Bible was in her hands. They each seemed to put different energies into their Bibles and received the same kind of energy from them in return.

As he tilted his head forward, Mira noticed the skin over her father's left ear, the sun filtering through the window behind him highlighting it. It dragged downward, the marking of a man with almost eighty years of gravity pulling at him. Faint age spots dotted his upper forehead, and though he still had most of his hair, it was thinner and wispier than it used to be in the back. She studied him for a moment, trying to absorb the reality that he was an "old man." That acknowledgment clearly made her less young than she used to be as well. But in that moment, with his Bible in his ill-working hands, he still projected paternal strength, at least to her.

When Matt saw his daughter enter, he smiled and labored to close the book, setting it on the table. It seemed that he had gone to great pains to lift it into position just under his nose for as long as he had. Mira sat on the couch and smiled back.

"Mom took Daniel out for a late lunch," he said. Mira was relieved. She didn't get to spend time alone with her father much anymore.

"I haven't been to synagogue in a long time," she said, gesturing toward his Bible. "I wouldn't even know what the *parsha* is this week." Mira had felt herself slipping away from ritual devotion for some time. Somewhere along the way it stopped serving her, and she lost faith in it. This was a personal rupture and Mira was careful never to deride religion more generally for its shortcomings. She was acutely aware that the shortcomings were entirely her own, and she forced herself to model active commitment while Lilly was living at home. She wanted her child to feel the connection she used to feel. Perhaps for her it would endure.

Sometimes, when Mira found herself at a friend's child's bar mitzvah or at a holiday table, the richness of what had drifted away from her came flooding back. It filled her up the way it used to, but only for a moment, and then it was gone again. It was painful, in the way her friends described the dissolution of their marriages where no ill will is involved, just estrangement. She wondered, when she looked at her father there with his Torah in his hands, how he managed to maintain his connection all his life.

"It is *Chayei Sarah*," Matt offered. "The Torah portion."

Mira thought for a moment and recalled the Bible story. "That's about Abraham sending his servant to find a wife for his son, Isaac, right?"

"Well!" he exclaimed with feigned joy, "I got my tuition's worth at that Jewish Day School we sent you to!"

Mira's eyes widened in playful shock as she looked at her father. "I really pulled that one out of the deep recesses of my mind. That may date back to the Third Grade!"

"Those were the good old days," he declared.

"When I was in the Third Grade?"

"No, ancient times. Why couldn't I be born at a time when a father marries his son off to a nice girl for a few camels? Daniel would be long settled by now."

Mira laughed again at the thought of her fastidious father even touching a camel. "You and tent-living don't seem like a fit," she teased him.

"True, but I wouldn't mind seeing Daniel settled in a rela-tionship, living a real life, at least before I die." He ended lots of sentences with "before I die."

"Dad, you know you have been planning your death for decades, right? Before you die is such an enormously long period of time by now that even something as outrageous and unlikely as Daniel Frank getting married is bound to happen within it."

Her father looked at her with what she thought might have been compassion. "Eventually, I will be right, you know."

She did know.

"Are you going to see Daniel at all while he is here?"

She didn't want to add drama to an already drama-filled week. "Of course," she said too quickly.

"Please, Mira, do," he pleaded.

She looked straight into her father's eyes. "I will, Dad. I will."

He took a deep breath. "I don't know what he is doing out there, Mira. I don't even ask questions anymore. We hardly talk. I am an ATM to him, I know. But I love him, and I would do anything for him. I won't be here forever." Matt trailed off. Mira wondered how any child of her father's could deny himself access to the gift of a relationship with him.

"I honestly don't know what he is up to out there either, Dad," she said. Mira saw the heartbreak on his face and refused to contribute to it, though she felt a fair amount of it herself. "But I think it is such a good sign that he is here," she said suddenly and with great enthusiasm. "I don't care what reason he gave for coming home. He is here because he was worried about you."

Matt smirked. "Yes," was all he said in response.

Mira looked at her father with her own dose of compassion. "Well, I am encouraged by that," she continued. "But I would also check your wallet before he goes," she added with a smile and a wink.

Matt chuckled. "Children are a luxury item!" he said, steering the conversation into lighter territory. He never wallowed for long. "Do you know what I spent on you all those years before marrying you off?" he asked as he had hundreds of times before. "If I had just been single and childless all my life, I would be on a yacht somewhere enjoying all the money I would still have."

Mira knew they had course corrected. "Wait, how did we pivot to me and how much I cost you? Anyway, it was money well-spent," she retorted as she always did. "I was worth every penny!"

Her father agreed. "Yes," he said, "you really were."

Mira's eyes began scanning the room and she noticed a new, brightly colored painting on the wall.

"Is that new? I haven't seen it before."

"Not only is it new, but it was free. I am married to the artist," Matt replied, smiling at his daughter, waiting for her reaction.

She jolted in her seat. "Wait, what? Mom painted that?"

"She did," he said proudly.

Mira got up and walked over to the painting for a closer look. It was an oil of a large, vividly colored flower. The hues were happy and evocative. It was the work of a skilled artist, and even more interestingly for Mira, it was the creation of someone with a joyful, artistic spirit. The work was so disconnected from the worker in Mira's mind that she had trouble imagining that her mother could have possibly produced it.

"I knew she was taking classes every day at that school in midtown, but I thought she was just trying to find some way to pass the time," Mira said, turning back to her father.

"Well, you know when I met her, she was always drawing and painting. I guess she just hasn't done anything with it for years."

"No, I didn't know that," Mira said, surprised. Nothing about her mother had ever suggested artistic aptitude. "She always loved museums. I remember she dragged us through all those endless 'mausoleums,' as Dan and I used to call them, during our Christmas-week trips to London when we were kids. But she always seemed more interested in the labels hanging next to the art than the art itself. It all seemed like an intellectual exercise with a backdrop of beauty. Inspector Clouseau wouldn't have guessed that she had creative flair and genuine artistic talent hidden within her. I am stunned."

"Go over to that cabinet over there, and open the middle drawer," Matt suggested. "Her folio is in there."

Mira did as instructed, pulling an oversized, leather-bound book out of the drawer. She sat back down on the couch with the book spread across her lap. There were at least thirty pages of paintings. She flipped each page one by one, and marveled at the collection of beautiful work.

She wondered about her mother's choice to suppress, over a lifetime, the kind of energy and enthusiasm she was witnessing in front of her. It could not have been too deeply buried, she surmised, given the burst of beauty she threw onto the page the moment she opened the floodgates. It struck Mira as much sadder than having no talent at all. Then she felt embarrassed for herself, for letting herself believe for so long that a child can ever really know her parent. She wondered, if asked, how Lilly would describe her.

"These are amazing," Mira finally said after looking through the folio for several minutes longer than it would have taken anyone else. "I can't believe I didn't know about this. I mean, I knew Lilly and Mom used to draw and paint together for hours, but I only ever saw what Lilly had made. It never occurred to me…"

Matt simply nodded.

"Dad," Mira said, shifting the conversation, and laying the folio down on the coffee table, "you seem to be getting more and more movement in your hands and arms. I don't think you could have held that book up to your face a week ago."

Matt looked at his daughter thoughtfully for a moment. "You know," he began, "I am used to being physically weak, but not helpless. It is a terrible thing to rely on someone else to button your pants." There was a joke in there about Velcro that Mira let pass.

"But I think Gloria likes that particular task," he added, unable to stop himself. "She has a crush on me." His condition may not have been funny, but it seemed worth laughing at anyway. Mira thought so too. What was the alternative? Crying wouldn't fix his fingers. Laughing would at least fix their mood.

"I don't know if I ever told you that my father had a minor heart attack about two years before the one that killed him," Matt said looking out the window.

"No, I don't think you ever did tell me that," she answered, interested.

"I actually don't remember now if it was a heart attack or a mini stroke," he continued, turning back to his daughter. "But he lost sight in his left eye as a result. I remember the fear he had of going completely blind after that. He lived with that overriding fear every single day. Sometimes I think that fear caused the subsequent heart attack that did kill him. I couldn't ever fully understand that kind of fear until my first operation. But even then, I was a young, healthy man. It was different. I am old now. I am an old guy with arms that don't work right anymore, and a sassy aide helping me brush my teeth. I know what my father felt. Life is a lot to get through. If you make it to old age, you should at least be rewarded with peace of mind and the ability to use the toilet on your own, and not necessarily in that order."

Matt wasn't seeking pity and he didn't need encouragement. He processed what was happening to him by talking about it, without the positive spin or the silver lining. Direct confrontation of the dark was his therapy.

They spent two hours together talking about politics, Mae, the opera, and the fondue they once had in the town of Gruyères on the way to Italy years ago. The time passed quickly and the afternoon light from the window started to change. Mira suddenly felt the desire to leave before Daniel and her mother came home. She wanted to leave the time with her father uninterrupted. She watched as he struggled to his feet, insisting he walk her to the door. After three tries he made it.

Gloria came in and pulled the walker in front of him. He grabbed onto the handles. "Thank you, Gloria."

The two made silent eye contact for a moment and there was an awkward pause. Mira braced for something, unsure what it would be.

Gloria put her hand on her chest and let out a cry of shock. "Lord, take me away!" she exclaimed. "This man thanked me for helping him. It's a miracle! I can die a happy woman!" She exited the room without another word.

Matt was gobsmacked. Mira saw it on his face. It was a mixture of approval, pleasant surprise, and respect. Gloria was here to stay.

~ ~ ~

It was cooler out now, and the air was crisp, so Mira decided to walk home. She started down Fifth Avenue, which was relatively quiet with little foot traffic. The sun was bright and obscured her view directly ahead, but she made out an irregular figure approaching from the opposite direction at a quick pace. Mira squinted and raised her hand to her brow to shade her eyes. She sensed there was something she needed to see.

The figure was a man walking rapidly with a briefcase in his hand and a cellphone to his ear. He was deeply engaged in conversation and looking about five paces in front of him as he moved steadily down the street. He would have been an other-wise unspectacular sight at four thirty on a Saturday afternoon in Manhattan, but this man was entirely naked, except for his shoes and a strategically placed surgical mask where Adam's fig leaf would have been.

He didn't screech or bark like many of the mentally ill home-less men she had become accustomed to in the city. He wasn't swerving or swaying, the telltale signs of the drug-addled class of men and women now all over the streets. He was entirely normal, but also entirely nude.

Mira startled a bit as he drew close and began to pass her to the left. She looked up to notice the few other people with her on the sidewalk seemingly oblivious to the shocking sight, their eyes riveted to the phones in their hands. Mira paused in place. She felt the moment needed to be absorbed.

Naked people roamed the Upper East Side, and she seemed to be the only one who cared. She turned to watch the naked little man walk up the street and felt a kind of despair overcome her. This, she thought to herself, was really not funny. All of civilization seemed to be falling apart right in front of her.

Just then, the doorman from the building up the street came a few feet out of his front door and yelled to the naked man, waving one arm in the air.

"Dude, does this look like the beach? Put some clothes on!" he bellowed.

He caught Mira's eye and winked, and her dread passed. The decline of the city was less terrifying once she knew she wasn't alone in watching it unfold. Then she laughed.

FLYPAPER

MIRA MET JENNA IN CENTRAL Park the next morning for their weekly walk around the reservoir. It was a beautiful early November morning, and the loop was busy with joggers. The two best friends met in a mommy-and-me music class sixteen years earlier. Mira had noticed she wasn't the only mother feigning delight while sitting in a circle and clapping along to forty-minutes of songs about happy dinosaurs. She shuffled over next to the other girl who was grinning and bearing it and a friendship was born.

Jenna was tall and lean with long, thick, brown hair, wide hazel eyes, and perfect posture. "Like a beauty pageant contestant being evaluated on stage," Mira used to tease her. She was a "head-turner" as Matt used to say, but she always led with her charm and brilliant sense of humor, never her looks. From the moment Mira met her, she loved her.

Jenna arrived at the park with her hair pulled down around her face to conceal the light bruising from her latest round of fillers. Her lips were swollen.

"You know, you are the only one I let see me this way," she said as she linked arms with Mira and started plowing ahead. Mira always felt like pleasant wallpaper next to her glamorous friend, but as they got older together, she felt the leveling effects of aging, which bothered Mira but tormented Jenna. Her beautiful friend, after all, had so much more to lose when the first frown lines set in.

Jenna fought back against the fading of her once unassailable beauty, often going too far. When she did, she laughed about looking like the "desperate old dame" she really was and made Mira promise to keep her away from the eyebrow tattooist for at least six more months. "We're all a little loopy," Jenna used to say, "but at least I admit it!"

"So, Jake and Lauren are divorced!" Jenna began as they walked.

"Wait, what?" Mira exclaimed in disbelief. "They loved each other! They held hands at dinner and looked at each other like they couldn't wait for the check to come so they could get home and be alone together!"

Jenna laughed. "Those couples are always the first to go," she said, dismissing Mira's naivete. "And did you hear what I said?! Divorced—not divorcing—*divorced*. It is already done. They sent out a Paperless Post announcement. When I got the email, I thought they were throwing a holiday party! Nope. Just a divorce announcement."

Mira was stunned. "Don't you have to suffer through years of legal fees and gossip and social isolation to get divorced anymore?" she asked, laughing.

Jenna threw her head back and giggled. "Right? Some of us paid our dues," she said with mock pride. "No one respects tradition anymore. When divorce becomes civilized, we know we are witnessing the fall of Western civilization."

As the women walked, the occasional passersby ogled Jenna. Even with bee-stung lips and nearly half-a-century of wear and tear, she still radiated something that men found irresistible. Mira told her it was her war-torn soul that others were attracted to. It was clear she wasn't just another pretty girl. She had lived through things, and that lit up her face better than a good shot of Botox.

They stopped briefly at the water fountain and as Jenna leaned over to take a drink, Mira saw an opening.

"Listen, I know you don't want to talk about it too much, and I am not asking for every detail, but how was it?"

Jenna stood up straight and smiled at her friend.

"Absolutely awful, actually," came the reply. "And I am fine talking about it with you. I want to." There was no hint of a quivering chin or a possible tear that might follow. It was a matter-of-fact review, characteristic of Jenna's approach to every one of her problems. And she had quite a few.

"Tell me," Mira prodded as they began walking again.

"Well, first of all, his area of Pennsylvania is…well, let's just say 'not pastoral.' I somehow thought I would get there, and it would be like a farm, with a charming house, a big porch—that sort of thing, you know? He lives in a little ranch house on a pretty average suburban-looking street in a town that lost about two-thirds of its population. It used to be a coal town, I think. It was sort of dark and depressing really. His wife was nice, I guess. After number three, I really stopped paying attention."

Mira jumped in. "How bad was he?"

Jenna again answered right away: "He had no idea who I was. When I reminded him that I was his daughter, he acted like it sounded familiar. It is much worse than she told me.

"I am so sorry J."

She shrugged off the sympathy. "There's nothing to be sorry about. I spent the next day filling out the admission papers and tipping the staff. I got him the room with the sitting area so it is more like a studio apartment. Anyway, it is dreary as can be. They have art classes and actual bingo night. It's a good thing I don't know him that well. If I did, I'm pretty sure I would know how much he hates art and bingo and then I would feel guilty subjecting him to them on Wednesdays and Fridays."

"Seriously," Mira started with supportive sympathy in her voice.

But Jenna cut her off. "Don't, Mira. I am no saint." It was always so interesting to Mira that a woman who clearly had been getting compliments all her life was so uncomfortable receiving them.

"Well, Jews don't have saints," Mira pointed out, "but if we did, a girl whose father left when she was twelve who has been supporting him and his fifth or sixth wife for the last three years while he descends further into Alzheimer's would be in the running."

Jenna shrugged. "Literally, there was no other choice," she said plainly, as if there weren't.

"Is your sister helping you at all? With logistics? Anything?" Mira asked.

"No. She just can't. Or won't. Maybe it's the same thing. Anyway, here is the funny thing, M, my dad was really a bad father and from what I can glean, not the best person. But the guy in Pennsylvania who stares into space most of the day and looks at me kindly when I help him out of his chair is clearly not my dad. This is a different person. This person hasn't left me or hurt me or disappointed me. So, this is who I am caring for and I am happy to do it. It is a sort of privilege really. If divorcing Bill had one upside, it was the financial ability to pay my ailing, old, Alzheimer's-riddled father's bills. I get to build a whole new relationship with this blank slate of a father, even if it is entirely one-directional."

Mira was listening, trying to understand, but she just couldn't. She knew Jenna had gotten a nice settlement in the divorce but not enough to support her and her father. The money she was spending on him was a sacrifice. More expensive than that was the emotional energy she devoted to someone who had never devoted any to her and now never could.

"You know, I have always admired your capacity for compassion, even though you didn't get much of it yourself growing up. I think it must be a quality best produced in people whose own needs were neglected."

"Right," Jenna joked in reaction to the compliment, "your father walks out on you and your mother chooses vodka over you, and you either become very compassionate or end up on the Investigation Discovery channel."

Mira pulled her elbow in and drew her friend a bit closer. Whenever she was lucky enough to find herself near human strength, she tried to pull it toward her.

Jenna changed the subject. "How is *your* dad doing?"

"Well," she replied, "he can move his fingers enough now to raise his middle one up when the mayor is on the news. So that's progress."

Jenna laughed. "Well, our mayor is just another reason to leave this city and head south. Have you decided about Miami?"

Mira had decided, but she hadn't found the courage to declare her decision to anyone. "No, not yet," she said, and they kept walking.

"So, tell me about the dating scene," Mira instructed, changing the subject to something she thought might be more uplifting. "What happened to Dr. Jim? Did you go out with him again?"

Jenna laughed out loud. "Oh, you mean Dr. Dread?" she exclaimed. "No, no second date."

Mira rolled her eyes. "What do you mean Dr. Dread?" she asked.

"That man must have gone to medical school just to be around death and illness, because he so clearly loves to talk about both," came the answer. "I have never been on a first date where the word 'hemangioma' was used and visuals were offered. I couldn't eat after he showed me the before and after pics of the surgery he performed."

Mira laughed. "Come on, he was trying to impress you. Don't bring down the ax because of that!"

Jenna shook her head. "You can't imagine. He talked endlessly about skin diseases and disorders. It was awful. And he couldn't read the room! My face was literally contorting in disgust, and he just kept on going as though he were captivating me with talk of broken capillaries. Never again."

"Come on! Sometimes, I think you must be kidding! Who raises these men? You should call his mother and file a complaint."

"Ha! Or maybe his ex-wife?" she suggested.

"Well, Mira said practically, "so he is not the one. Next."

"Next?" Jenna repeated sarcastically. "I am a single woman in my late forties with crepey skin forming on my knees. 'Next' might be three years from now and seventy-three-years-old. That is what is out there."

Now Mira was shaking her head. "You sound like such a cliché!" she admonished her friend. "I know good men are hard to find, blah blah blah, but you aren't just another forty-something-year-old woman, Jenna. You are flypaper to men. There will always be a 'next' for you. Girls like me, on the other hand, would sooner murder our husbands than divorce them, because we understand exactly what awaits us in the dating market."

Jenna's pace slowed a bit. She looked at Mira adoringly. "My amazing, beautiful friend, you don't see yourself. And you don't understand that because you were so loved by that incredible father of yours, you drew that incredible husband to you. And ten others would line up behind him to take his place. You know what it is to love and be loved by a man. That is the real flypaper."

Mira smiled uncomfortably. "Okay, no more of this mushy, sentimental stuff. I am no better at it than you are. If you want to compliment something, tell me what you think of my new Dior sneakers."

Jenna pulled Mira in closer now as they continued on.

DANIEL

THAT NIGHT, MIRA MET DANIEL at the Italian restaurant around the corner. She had texted him after the promise she made to her father. It was a quiet spot and Mira knew Daniel loved the burrata salad there. She wanted him to be happy.

Mira was already seated when she saw her brother enter. As he checked his coat and walked the long length of the restaurant toward her, she noticed more than one female diner turn and glance with interest at him as he moved down the center aisle. She smiled to herself, imagining Daniel through the eyes of these admirers. They saw a handsome man, one who still radiated so much vitality and potential.

But there had been so much more. These women were eyeing the shadow of her brother; they were enamored by the trail of light that lingered from before.

They couldn't know how bright that light once was. Daniel was magnetic once upon a time. His sense of humor was brilliant, emerging from the great intellect he naturally possessed, but it was also accessible and light. He shared his charisma and his energy with others effortlessly, as though he were a bottomless well that would never dry up. Everyone loved him for it, Mira most of all. She was proud of her brother for a moment, thinking others could still see a hint of who he used to be.

"Hello," he said casually as he sat down across from his sister.

"Hi there," Mira said, trying to sound breezy, not getting up.

She looked at him and remembered how much she missed him, especially when she was with him. The man in front of her looked ill at ease and anxious, like he hadn't really felt unburdened for a long time. She felt sorry for him for the loss of the gift he had somehow suffered. And more so for herself, realizing how much she had benefited from Daniel's old nature while he still had it to share.

Now she was the one pumping cheer into the room when they were together, and she was nowhere near as good at it as Daniel used to be. She made small talk for as long as she could. She showed him a few pictures of Lilly and talked about Mae. She referenced their father's surgery and slow recovery only once to see if her brother would pursue that conversation, but he didn't. There were too many awkward silences that lingered in the air and Mira suffered through each one desperately. She would have been happier to argue with her brother than to not have a thought as to what to say to him.

Halfway through the main course, Daniel held his fourth drink in his hand and started playing with his bread knife with his right. He cleared his throat and asked Mira a question. It was the only conversation he had initiated thus far.

"Hey, are you and Aaron moving to Miami or not? Weren't you going to leave by the end of the year?" he asked abruptly.

Mira was startled that he remembered. When she mentioned it to her brother all those months ago, he had been in Los Angeles for a short time with plans to return to New York at some point in the future. He hadn't caught on to the fact that

Mira was searching for some sign that he might consider being in the city to be near their parents if she were to leave. Or maybe he did and didn't want to entertain the idea of it. He never brought it up again. Neither did she.

"Well," Mira began, adjusting in her seat, "the truth is that I liked the idea a lot. I love Miami, and Aaron was eager to go."

Daniel interrupted with interest. "*Was?*"

Mira tried to read his expression, but she had lost that ability with her brother years ago. "Well," she continued, "I think Aaron and I both understand that I just can't leave now." He was the first person she had told.

Daniel replied quickly, as though he had practiced this conversation in his head before. He seemed agitated, but Mira wasn't sure. "Why not? Why can't you leave now?" he asked, almost accusatorily.

Mira could feel herself being led into something that she probably didn't want to engage, but the question bothered her. It suggested a judgment she didn't feel this particular judge was in a position to make.

"Dad needs me, Daniel," she said with some annoyance in her voice. "He is getting older and weaker. You saw him. I can't just leave him and Mom here alone. *Obviously.*" With that last word she knew she had pushed the button that had been waiting to be pushed.

"What does 'obviously' even mean?" Daniel said, his voice rising. "To you, maybe. Not to anyone else." Now, he had a haughty tone that truly irritated Mira. "Dad isn't a kid," he continued, "and it isn't your job to give up your life for your parents." He spoke too angrily. He was rude and dismissive, and Mira was startled at first. She wondered how long he had been waiting to say this to her.

She persuaded herself that he hadn't intended to sound so biting. The tone she heard directed at her was really the voice he likely had swirling around in his head, self-loathing and bitter. She felt sorry for him when she thought about it.

She used the next few moments of silence to collect her racing thoughts and choose her response carefully. She spoke to her brother slowly and with a softer tone. "I am not giving up my life for anyone, Daniel, that's a bit of an overstatement, don't you think?" she said, hoping to take the drama out of the conversation and de-escalate.

It didn't work. He was smirking now, which enraged her. "Not living where you want to live because you can't cut the cord is probably the definition of 'giving up your life,' actually," he snapped back. "You made this your job. *Obviously.*"

That was it for Mira. She wasn't about to accept advice about caring for their parents from someone who hadn't done much of it himself. She was more than angry, she was indignant. All the time that Daniel had been out in California and didn't call to say hello or to see how she was, Mira assumed he wasn't thinking about her at all. She imagined he was entirely self-absorbed and hadn't given her life five minutes of serious consideration. Now, she realized that he *was* thinking about her, and judging her, and in the most unkind way. She wondered how he felt he even had the right to offer his assessment of her choices, given the fact that he had absented himself from her life to such a large degree for so long. It was intolerable.

"Whose job is it then, Daniel?" she said, her own voice rising. "Yours?" She scoffed, wanting to shame him, hoping he would feel ashamed. But she knew he wouldn't, at least not enough to change anything. She stared at him for a long moment and edited out her next thoughts about Daniel and jobs. Even now, she was still careful with him.

Then she continued. "Is it a job to be there for family? Is that how you see it? Well, I don't." Mira stopped again. She never broke eye contact, so he would know every word she said was considered and deliberate. "Sometimes it is hard. Sometimes it is an inconvenience, that is true. But what you aren't considering is that it is also…my privilege." She summoned Jenna's word and it fit so perfectly. "You don't want to burden yourself? So don't. Believe me, no one expects you to anymore. But don't project whatever it is you are going through on me. You have no idea what you are talking about."

Daniel was agitated by the response, not willing to concede, but also not willing to engage anymore. "Okay, whatever," he said dismissively, as though he were an expensive therapist offering his finest advice to a stubborn patient determined to ignore it. "I was just trying to help you. You don't understand."

Mira wasn't sure what to say. It wouldn't have taken Sigmund Freud to point out that Daniel was clearly trying to help himself feel better, not his sister. That wasn't new. But could someone who had excused himself from life the way Daniel had really sit across from her as she tried her best to contend with it and tell her she didn't understand? She thought for a moment that this was one of those great moments where you get to choose whether to laugh or cry. She did what her father would have done.

She pulled back from her aggressive posture leaning across the small table and leaned back in her chair. "Anyway, I can't live in Florida," she said lightly, looking down at the flickering candle on the table rather than at her brother. "I would never have a good hair day again. And what would I do with all my great coats?"

Daniel didn't laugh. He just wrapped his hand around his glass and gently shook his head as though he had to resign himself to the idea that he had tried to help Mira, but she just wouldn't help herself. If Mira had thought for a moment that his sanctimony was real and not a deflection, she would have been even more furious. But she knew better, so she tried another approach.

"You know," she began in a soft, calm voice, "when Grandma was dying, I went down to Florida to say goodbye. Dad had been there for a week already and he looked so tired. She had twenty-four-hour care, but he hardly left her side."

Daniel leaned back in his chair and listened.

"One afternoon, I sent Dad back to his hotel to get some sleep and I sat with grandma. She was full of morphine. They had put her in a large recliner and she was half-sitting up and half-lying back. Her eyes were open, but she was glassy-eyed and distant—non-responsive. I was talking to her even though I didn't know if she could really hear me. I told her about Lilly and Aaron, and I filled her in on all the news headlines I knew she would have wanted to know about. You know, she always read everything."

Mira paused to evaluate her brother's interest level. She still couldn't read his expression, so she continued.

"Suddenly, her eyes changed, Dan. They seemed to focus in on me, and there was what I can only describe as life behind them. Then, out of nowhere, she opened her mouth and said,

'Every now and then, buy your father a tie.' That was it. Just as suddenly, her eyes glazed over again, and she was far away. It was unbelievable."

Daniel still sat stoically.

"Under any other circumstances and with any other grand-mother, I would not have believed my own eyes. But somehow it didn't seem that crazy to think that Grandma's spirit had been halfway between this world and the next, and that she came back for a few fleeting seconds to deliver an order. If anyone was going to break through the earthly-heavenly divide to get an important task done, it would be her. You know what she was like."

Daniel didn't scoff. Mira took that as a small victory, as well as an opportunity to continue, and make her point.

"Grandma wasn't the most doting and maternal of moth-ers, though of course, she loved Dad. She was so busy with her work, and for a woman at that time, she had to really fight for every accomplishment. She was away a lot, not home-cooking dinner and tucking him in. I think, as she got older, she had a lot of regrets. He did everything for her in her old age, and in some sense, I think she thought it was an unearned privilege—an incredible gift. She was asking me to take care of him, in the way she hadn't, to repay that gift. I guess you could say I felt like she deputized me. And I take that responsibility seriously—not just because she asked me, but because Dad has always taken care of me too. I also feel like I have been given an unearned gift. I have a debt to repay as well."

Mira didn't go on about additionally wanting to be there for her father because she loved him and enjoyed his company. She edited her story for her audience, choosing the part she thought her brother might relate to. She waited for the big breakthrough, but it didn't come.

Daniel just looked at her blankly and said, "Okay."

Astonished by his non-reaction, Mira just stared at her brother. He was unrecognizable now, such that she wondered if she had dreamed up the person she remembered him to be. She had worked up the nerve to ask him years ago if he did any serious drugs just after college. She thought perhaps he had used something that altered his brain chemistry, so dramatic was the shift in his personality. He looked startled by the question as though Mira's search for an answer to the mystery of his transformation came out of nowhere. He assured her that drugs were not his problem, but never explained what was. She stopped probing after a while, because she knew her obvious disapproval hurt Daniel and that he stayed away from her mostly to avoid feeling it. She wondered if he knew that she avoided him because her disappointment in him broke her heart.

All these years, she had genuinely missed her brother and their relationship. Now, she couldn't remember what it was that she missed. As her parents aged, though, she knew she longed for a reliable sibling with whom to navigate their growing list of needs. Just an able body and an extra set of willing hands would have been nice.

It had been too quiet for too many minutes, so Mira made an absurd request. "If you could visit more often, it really would help, Dan," she said, as though it were even remotely likely that he would visit more, or true that it would help if he did. She wanted him to feel useful even if he wasn't. She sensed he needed to hear that he might be. Maybe she needed to believe he could be. "It would be nice to know someone is here to pitch in when we are away, you know."

Daniel nodded a bit but just continued to stare down at his drink.

Mira took a deep breath. "Daniel," she began, "I can't leave Mom and Dad now. I don't want to. I couldn't enjoy being in Miami with them here like this. Aaron understands. It's fine. It's what I want. Really." She looked at her brother and her heart just kept breaking.

Daniel shrugged and made an unintelligible sound. "Okay, whatever," he mumbled as he fiddled with his napkin. He clearly was done with this conversation. As the check came, Mira sensed she wasn't going to see her brother for a while, so she thought she would ask something that was on her mind.

"Daniel, why did you come to New York this week?" she asked gently. He looked solemn, she thought, but she couldn't really tell.

He shook his head and just said, "I don't know."

~ ~ ~

Mira came home and found Aaron in the same position she had left him, with reduced stacks of paper on his desk and a half-eaten tuna sandwich from the diner next to him. She placed the small plastic container of biscotti she brought home from the restaurant in front of him and he lit up when he saw it.

Mira sat down on the couch. "I'm sorry," she said.

Aaron looked at her, surprised. "For what?" he asked.

"For ever thinking I might agree to move. For letting you think it was possible all this time. For not telling you months ago there was no way I would ever be able to do it. I can't leave my parents."

He was quiet, then rolled himself over to her on his office chair until they were knee-to-knee. "Mira, it really is fine," he said sincerely. "It is more than that, actually. It is right. And I admire you for it."

She let out a small laugh. "Ha, that is exactly what Daniel just said! Great minds..."

WHAT WILL WE DO
WITHOUT THEM?

MIRA WAS AT MAE'S APARTMENT the next day setting up her laptop on the small kitchen table. There were papers strewn everywhere and as she collected them to move them out of the way, she saw that they were sketches of the Brooklyn Bridge, done in pencil. One after the other they were beautiful, skillfully done, and unfinished. Some had large black "X" marks drawn through them. One was ripped in half. She carefully placed them in a neat pile in the corner where they wouldn't be disturbed.

She went to get Mae from her bedroom and sat her down in front of the screen. "Okay, we're going to give this a try," she said excitedly, wondering why she hadn't thought to organize a Zoom call for Mae and her father before. When Aaron mentioned it, she stopped in her tracks and gasped at her failure to have thought of the obvious. Aaron laughed and said she shouldn't be so hard on herself—it wasn't really that obvious to think of technology and her father in the same sentence.

Mae sat as instructed, but still wasn't sure what Mira had been talking about. She said they were going to call Matt, but she didn't see a phone. Mira sat next to her, logged into Zoom, and waited for Gloria to sign her father in from his apartment in

Manhattan. The alert sounded, and he was in the waiting room. She hit the "Admit" button and Matt's confused face appeared, too close to the screen, filling it up almost entirely.

"Move back a bit, Dad," she said as she positioned the camera on herself and Mae.

"Back?" he yelled, not understanding. "Back where?"

She laughed. "You don't have to yell, Dad. This isn't a tin can with a string. Just speak normally. Move back a few inches. We can see every pore. Can you see us?"

Matt looked amused. He had used Zoom a few clumsy times before but was always amazed by the technology. "Yes!" he exclaimed as though it were a miracle that he could. "I see you!"

Mae squinted at first through her thick-lensed glasses. Her mouth hung open a bit as she leaned in toward the computer, astonished. "Matthew?" she said as loudly as she could. "Matt, is that you, child?" she yelled again while lightly reaching her finger out toward the screen in amazement.

"You don't have to yell," Mira said gently in her ear, demonstrating the correct volume level for her voice. "You just speak normally, as though Dad were here with you at the table."

"Who are you calling a child?" Matt laughed.

Mae shook her head and cried out with awe at a world she couldn't imagine but found herself in. "Lord, have mercy!" was all she could say. Mira beamed with delight at the accomplishment. She watched each of their faces as the two old friends looked at each other and laughed at the absurdity and wonderfulness of it all. It took a minute before they could recover themselves and begin to talk.

Before long, Mae and Matt had stopped yelling into their screens and settled into a comfortable and familiar conversation that spanned family, old memories, the Bible, and life. Mae's first concern was of course his health. She prayed over him, and Mira could see how deeply she meant every word. She thought that if God were in the business of answering prayers, He wouldn't have the heart to deny Mae hers.

Mira went to the other side of the room and pretended to be checking her emails to give her father and Mae some semblance of privacy, but she was listening to every word of their conversation as though it were a beautiful and tragic aria. She swelled with emotion at the sound of it. As Mae spoke, Mira raised her phone and snapped a picture of her with the computer and sent it to Lilly with a caption that read, "You're never too old to become a tech wizard!"

As she listened to the voices of the two people who had anchored her life since she was born riffing off one another, back and forth, a wave of awareness came over her that halted her breath. *This is as good as life will ever be*, she thought silently to herself. It was a surprise to have that awareness in a tiny, run-down Brooklyn apartment rather than standing on a beach or at the top of a mountain, but great realizations don't always happen in great surroundings, she thought. *My family is healthy, my parents are alive, Mae is alive, everyone is safe. This is a moment I will look back on and wish I could get back. It won't stay this way.*

It was a terrible thought, but it pleased her to have recognized it and taken the moment to absorb it in all its beauty and cruelty. She would have hated to face the decline of the world that had sustained her without having stopped to notice the moments before it began. She thought then of Daniel and wished she could remember the last time she and he were belly-laughing together on the couch watching old Tim Conway clips on his iPad. But she couldn't.

Her thoughts were interrupted when she heard Mae ask about Daniel. "How was his visit?" she asked.

"I honestly don't know, Mae," her father said. "He barely said three words to me the whole time he was here. I don't think he likes being around me very much."

Mae wouldn't hear it. "That boy just need time," she said. "You need to pray on it," she said.

"I don't understand it," he said with sadness in his voice. "What I haven't done for him! I have done everything I can for him. I don't know how to make him happy."

Mae looked at Matt and reproached him as only she could. "Matthew, you know God Himself don't make most people happy. Why do you think you are supposed to? You just got to love that boy, love your son, and let God touch him."

He nodded in resigned agreement as Mira committed those words of wisdom to memory.

"How is Willie's daughter doing?" Matt asked. Mira perked up and listened intently.

"God is good," Mae replied. "She move to Georgia last week for that job at the college. She doin' good. Praise the Lord."

"I knew she would recover," Matt said. "Thank God. She is a bright girl."

Mira never knew Willie had a child. Recover? From what? She looked over at Mae and realized suddenly how much she didn't know.

~ ~ ~

It was two days before Thanksgiving and Mira sat in Nick's chair again. The salon was buzzing with women rushing to get their color and cuts before the holiday. Nick was sitting on a stool behind Mira. He could no longer stand because of the pain from the herniated disk in his back. He had delayed getting surgery for a year. The two talked pain management for a time, Mira being something of an expert-adjacent because of her father. He had always refused most pain management protocols, but at some point, over the years, she had carefully investigated every one of them.

"Well," Nick said finally, "I am definitely going to get a cortisone shot tomorrow before my mother arrives. Nothing is more painful than the look of concern on your eighty-year-old parent's face when she sees you hurting, right?!"

Mira nodded emphatically, in total agreement.

"Yeah," he said laughing. "I know you know what I mean. My mother is Italian. Your father is Jewish. On the worry-Richter scale, they are about even when it comes to their kids. Never lower than an eight-point-five."

Truer words had never been spoken, she thought.

As he painted over her roots, he told her about the four different main courses he had been cooking for the last week because turkey alone wouldn't cut it at an Italian-Catholic Thanksgiving table. His elderly mother, whom he adored, would be staying with him through the weekend. It was funny, Mira thought to herself, that he called his eighty-year-old mother "elderly." Her father wasn't far behind in age, but it never occurred to her to use that word to describe him.

"So, I gotta tell you the funniest story about my mother," Nick started. Mira was already smiling. "Every year after the holiday, I take her shopping for a new Christmas dress. It is our tradition. That woman is eighty years old and has arthritis and is usually exhausted from cooking and cleaning after Thanksgiving dinner, but she is up, dressed, and ready to go by nine o'clock the next day. No one loves a sale like my mother," he began.

He was rolling around on his stool, painting away at her head, while talking. His hands were enormous, matching the rest of his body which looked like that of a retired football player who still had a large, muscular frame underneath thirty extra pounds accumulated over the years. Mira had never met his mother, but she pictured a tiny little lady conjured up from another era who babied her sixty-year-old only son, the sight of whom somehow belied the thought that he even had a mother. She imagined most people seeing Nick walking down a dark alley at night would have crossed the street in fear of the looming figure he was. They didn't know his mommy still knit him scarves.

"So, I know my mother," he continued. "She still thinks the bus costs seventy-five cents. She isn't price-adjusted to the last forty years," he chuckled. "But she loves this brand, St. John. Know it?" Mira said that she did. "They make those little knit suits with the gold buttons," he continued, "and Mom loves them. But they are definitely priced for 2022! Holy crap!" He was getting louder and more animated as he told the story. The women to the left and the right of Mira were now listening as well.

"The first time we went in there, years ago, my mother fell in love with this royal blue knit thing with a black bow. She looked at the price tag and I could see that she just couldn't compute. I swear I thought I saw smoke coming out of her ears. I called over the saleswoman and asked her to confirm the discount price because of the big holiday sale. I wasn't sure she got it at first, but she did, luckily. She took the suit to the back and returned a few minutes later saying they hadn't had time to mark things down yet, but instead of $2,000, the suit was now $499. We saved Mom from a stroke, I could see."

He paused for dramatic flourish, rolled his chair around to the other side of Mira's head and continued. "But $500 for a suit was still a small fortune to a lady who remembered when cars cost that much. So, I whipped my credit card out of my pocket along with a piece of paper and handed it to the saleswoman and said we'd take it and could she also please add this coupon I had for $200. I winked at her, and she took them and went to the back again where she charged me the full price. She was smart enough to slide the receipt into my hand as she handed the bag to mom.

"Every year since, I take Mom back there and that same woman is so nice. She pulls five or six outfits she knows Mom will like and writes an acceptable price on the tag with a black marker. And I bring her a 'coupon.' And Mom is a sharp-dressed lady on New Year's Eve!"

"Oh, that is just sweet," Mira said, impressed. "Sweet of you and sweet of that saleswoman!"

Nick laughed. "Yes, but the story continues!" he said loudly, as everyone was now riveted and listening in. Half the salon was his audience.

"This past year was a tough one financially for me and Dave, and Mom knows it. We are fine, but we took a hit in the market. So, for my birthday last month I get a card in the mail from my mother with a check for $2,000 in it. In the card she writes, *Happy Birthday to my son. You are a good boy and a bad liar. I have known for ten years that St. John doesn't make coupons!* I almost fell over! What is she going to do if she ever figures out that St. John also doesn't sell suits for $500?"

He was laughing out loud now. So was everyone else around them. Mira's mouth fell open.

"What a character!" she exclaimed in deep appreciation of Nick's mother and her methods. "What would you ever do without her?" she asked.

He rolled up next to her and put his head close to hers, staring at her straight in the mirror. With deep love, and equal parts foreboding, he replied, "I honestly don't know."

Mira's phone rang. When she looked down and saw her mother's name, she thought God couldn't be that obvious, so the lump in her throat softened as she answered. "Mom?"

"Mira, Mae is in the hospital," Dana said quickly. Mira could hear her father in the background on his phone talking to someone about a hospital room.

"What happened?" she asked as though Mae weren't an old, homebound woman, unwell for years.

"She was apparently coughing a lot. Willie said she was coughing up blood. He called 911. They brought her to the emergency room at Interfaith Medical Center in Brooklyn and she is stable now. Dad is arranging for a private transfer to Columbia Presbyterian where we can get her a private room and a nurse."

Dana paused for a moment and Mira could hear a sigh on the other end of the line. "Maybe we can get some kind of a frequent flier discount at that place. We use it enough, unfortunately. Anyway," her mother said, snapping back into business mode, "we will call you back when we know more." She hung up before Mira could respond.

"Okay, thanks," Mira said to herself and the thin air.

She hadn't heard anything more, so on the way home from the salon, she stopped at her parents' apartment. She went straight to her father in the living room and asked for the update.

"Mae is being brought to Columbia," he said. He had clearly been working on logistics for the last hour. "I couldn't get Alice to look in on her. She is off today. But I luckily got a night nurse to show up at eight o'clock, and she will stay with her overnight just so she isn't alone. I wanted to go myself, but Mom said I just couldn't. I should wait until tomorrow," he reported, looking at his daughter for confirmation he had gotten the right instructions.

"No, you can't go now, Dad. It's too much for you. You go tomorrow. Should I go? I can run up there." She wanted to go, and not just for her father.

"Mira, you have a lot of people coming over in two days and there is nothing you can do right now for Mae, anyway. I don't even know if they will let you in at this hour," he said, checking his watch. "I don't want you going up there alone at night. Wait until tomorrow and we can go together, okay?"

She wanted to relieve him of any more worry, so she agreed.

~ ~ ~

The next day, Mira met her parents at their apartment early. They wanted to be at the hospital when visiting hours opened. Matt had organized a car service and requested a sedan, knowing he would never be able to get in and out of an SUV.

They walked to the waiting car slowly, Matt holding on to his walker, which the driver took from him and folded into the trunk. Dana went directly into the back and Mira stood with her father at the opened passenger door.

Matt seemed to evaluate the height of the seat and the handle over the window, calculating his next move. He shook his head and called to the driver to return his walker to him. Grabbing the handles of the walker, he positioned himself with his back to the car opening and locked the walker in place in front of him. He motioned as though he were leaning back to sit down and then stopped, judging the descent into the seat to be too difficult. He had no core strength to control the motion, and his back muscles were too weak to brace him. Then he placed one hand on the walker and the other on the internal handle of the car trying to reposition himself more advantageously but aborted that plan just as quickly.

Mira stood next to her father, equally frustrated, and asked how she could help.

After a moment of silence, Matt responded dejectedly. "I can't," he said softly. "Even if I get in, how will I get out?" he said almost to himself. The look of misery on his face made her determined to solve the problem.

"Dad, let me get your seat cushion from upstairs," she offered. "It will elevate the seat height and make it easier to get in."

"No, Mira, I realize now this was never going to work. I just wanted to see Mae so badly. It was my mistake. I am making you and your mother late. You two go without me," he said.

It was a cruel moment, she thought. She could read her father's mind. He was thinking this might be his last chance to ever see Mae face to face and he couldn't get his old broken body into a car. He headed back slowly with his walker to the front door and through the lobby. The doorman escorted him.

Mira waited until she saw her father safely in the elevator headed back upstairs before getting back into the car with her mother who never said a word.

The same lobby with the preserved, sad bouquets of flowers in the gift shop greeted them when they arrived at the hospital. The two women found their way up to the fifth floor where Mae's room was.

The doctor was already there, along with two of his students. They had been saying something to Mae who was awake and looking at them blankly. Mira rushed to Mae's side and stood next to her, facing the medical team gathered at the foot of the bed. She introduced herself and asked the doctor to repeat everything he had just told Mae, so she and her mother could hear it all.

"We did a chest X-ray and a CT scan," he began. "There are no signs of cancer or tumors. No pneumonia or bronchitis. We believe it was just inflammation and irritation of the airways." He then looked at Mae. "Ms. Boyd," he began slowly and loudly, "have you been sick lately? Any flu?" She didn't answer. Her eyes were sunken and glazed over a bit. She shook her head gently. The doctor then turned to Mira. "We want to monitor her for twenty-four hours and make sure there is no recurrence. If everything checks out, we should be able to discharge her tomorrow and she can go home," he said.

Mira thanked the doctor and he and his team left.

"Mae, how are you feeling?" she asked, bending over the bed. She held Mae's hand to let her know she was there. Even though her eyes were open, and she was responsive, she seemed somewhere else entirely.

Suddenly, Mae turned her head toward Mira and focused in on her. She smiled weakly. "God is good, Mira," she said. "Don't you worry about me." Then she turned to Dana. "He is in charge. You have to praise Him."

Dana had been standing in the corner of the room near the entrance the entire time. She had let her daughter take over and watched quietly as she did. The first thing she said was, "Let's call Matt, okay?"

She pulled out her phone and started dialing. "Daniel taught me how to use Facetime," she said proudly as she approached the bed on the other side from Mira and held the phone in front of Mae who seemed a bit confused. Gloria picked up and turned the phone on Matt.

When Mae saw him, she laughed. "Praise the Lord!" she exclaimed.

Mira told her father what the doctor said, and he was relieved.

"Mae, tomorrow is Thanksgiving," Matt reminded her. "Don't go home. Please. Come here and stay with us for the weekend," he pleaded. He wanted to see her, and he was afraid to let her go back to her apartment where she wouldn't be looked after the way she would be in the Frank home.

Mae seemed fully present now. "Matt," she said solidly, "I am goin' home."

Matt never took no for an answer, so he kept pleading. "Mae, do it for me," he begged her. "I can't get up those stairs to see you. I need you here, please."

There was nothing she wouldn't do for him, but she stopped him before he continued on. "Matthew," she said, before a long pause. "Matthew, child, I am goin' home. You understand?"

He nodded, confirming that he did. Mira did as well, and she felt a lump in her throat. Matt simply said, "I understand. I do."

Dana interrupted. "Mae, you know what I was thinking about just now? Your turkey stuffing. We haven't had it in years. No one makes stuffing like you do." Mae's recipe was legendary. Unfortunately, it was also never written down. She had tried to teach Dana and then Mira, but it never tasted like the original no matter how hard they tried. They had both long ago decided that rather than produce something second rate, they would simply cherish the first-rate memory of a dish that belonged to another chef.

Mae's face lit up, and so did Matt's. "Mira, remember when you first discovered that she put chopped-up liver in there after you had been eating it for years," he recalled.

She laughed, "It was a crushing blow! Ignorance is definitely bliss. Liver!" she recalled, recreating the shocked and horrified face of the fifteen-year-old girl who first discovered the unappetizing news about her favorite food.

"I ain't stuttin' 'bout you, girl!" Mae almost bellowed, her voice now stronger. "You ate that liver, and a bunch of other stuff I ain't *never* told you 'bout noways."

Mira looked at Mae, then at her father. "What? Dad, what does she mean? What else did she put in my food that I don't know about?"

Matt simply smiled. Dana looked at her daughter. "Remember the hamburgers she used to make every Sunday night? Well, she fried them in schmaltz." She hardly finished speaking before bursting into laughter.

Mira was at first stunned at the sight of her mother laughing so hard, then at the recognition that her parents had kept a secret, any secret, from her. Then, she realized that she had been eating poultry fat all throughout her childhood.

"Ugh," she said with her hand on her chest, "Good thing we are in a hospital. I may pass out."

The four of them laughed and reminisced for a while before the nurse came in to run a few more tests. Matt said his goodbyes and Mira and Dana went to the front desk to make arrangements for private nursing and an ambulette service home for Mae when she was discharged. The attendant said Willie had volunteered to come to the hospital to sign her out and escort her home. Mira and her mother were happy to hear it, but they wouldn't leave the logistics up to him.

As they were leaving, Mira arranged for a food delivery that evening from Mae's favorite local restaurant, *For Goodness Steak*, so her kitchen would be stocked for the long weekend. She made sure to order lots of meat and pasta dishes, and some lighter meals for Mae as well.

Mira and Dana didn't say much on the way home. They drove south on the West Side Highway and both of them stared out the windows. The river never stopped moving and the long running and bike path along the length of it didn't either. There were people everywhere enjoying the day before the holiday, jogging, and strolling with their families. Mira noticed a toddler sitting on a bench by the water, holding her mother's hand, laughing.

She thought about Mae's hand when she held it at the hospital. It had no volume, age having removed every ounce of unneeded flesh. Her fingers were bony and the skin was like thin, wet paper draped loosely over the skeletal structure. She held her hand like a psychic holding a missing person's jacket, trying to conjure up the scent of something those left behind were searching for.

"I got up early this morning and made Mae's stuffing," Dana said, interrupting Mira's thoughts. "It won't be as good as hers, but we have to try to keep that recipe alive," she said, staring out her window as well.

Mira knew that recipe took Mae at least three hours to make. Her mother must have been up since four o'clock in the morning. She wanted to ask her mother something, but she couldn't exactly figure out what it was. She was startled by the thought that her reaction to Mae's hospitalization was to hold on to some piece of her, even if it was just a recipe.

"How are we going to get Dad over to my place tomorrow?" she asked, changing the subject.

"I don't know," Dana replied. "But he will be there," she said definitively.

She decided to let her mother handle this one.

NOT FUNNY

WHEN SHE GOT HOME, MIRA opened the door and Lilly was there waiting for her.

"Surprise!" she yelled.

Mira grabbed her daughter and hugged her. She had to stand on her tiptoes to reach her. With her hands still grasping her daughter's arms, she stepped back to look at her, overcome. "I am un-surprisable! How in the world did you manage this?" she asked joyfully.

"Well, clearly not," laughed Lilly. "Actually, you are so surprisable—it was easy."

Mira and Aaron sat down with their daughter in the kitchen the way the three of them all had before Lilly left for school. "How long are you here for?" Mira asked. She was still getting used to asking her child that question, still trying to accept that she didn't live at home anymore.

"I am going back Sunday," she said.

"Great!" she tried to sound breezy when she then asked what plans Lilly made for the weekend. She didn't want her daughter to hear in her voice the desperate hope that she hadn't made any plans at all, and that Lilly could spend every minute with her.

"Just Saturday night with friends. Oh, and Grandma and I are going to do some painting Friday morning. Then I thought maybe you and I could go out for lunch, do a little shopping?"

Mira answered too quickly but she couldn't help herself. "Yes!" she blurted out. Aaron chuckled.

Mira thought for a second and then realized that her parents had known about the surprise too. "Did the doorman also know you were coming home for the weekend?" she asked, laughing at herself, still shocked that she was the last to know.

"Oh, and I thought maybe we would all go to synagogue Saturday morning," Lilly added. She saw the surprise on her parents' faces. "I mean, I have been going to services on campus and I kind of like it," she continued more tentatively. "You don't have to—I just thought...."

Mira pulled back in her seat and looked at her daughter with appreciation for the gift that she was. "Have to?" she exclaimed, turning to face her husband. "Aaron, do you think a parent could wish for anything more than her teenage daughter to ask her if it is okay if they go to synagogue together?" Then she looked again at Lilly and squinted as she spoke. "Don't you know you are supposed to come home from school and tell your parents that you are now a Wiccan and a Communist who resents everything about the narrow way you were raised? What have they done to you at that school? Aren't you taking gender studies classes and being brainwashed like everyone else?"

Aaron stopped her. "Don't jinx us!" he cautioned. "And don't even suggest to our daughter that taking a Gender Studies class is something we would pay for!"

Lilly blushed a little. "I know—synagogue. But I like it...." She let her sentence trail off again.

"I love that you like it!" Mira said, filled with admiration for her daughter who surpassed her in every conceivable character trait that mattered. "And all evidence to the contrary aside, since

I don't go much anymore, I think I like it too. I think it is exactly what I want to do this weekend."

"How is Mae?" Lilly finally asked.

"She isn't doing well," Mira answered honestly. "She is hopefully going home tomorrow. But she isn't doing well." Lilly reached over and held her mother's hand. "I am sorry, Mom," she said. "What can I do?"

Mira smiled at her daughter and squeezed her hand. "You are already doing it."

~ ~ ~

Thursday morning was a storm of activity in the Cayne apartment. Lilly had gone out for a run. She was the only college kid Mira knew who didn't sleep until noon. Mira was busy setting the table and organizing the chairs. There would be sixteen people for Thanksgiving dinner. She reconfirmed that her parents were coming first thing that morning. She could hear the hesitation in her father's voice but she cut him off by telling him Aaron would be over shortly to pick up his chair and seat cushion so he would be comfortable. The Baums were coming as was Dr. Baron, Aaron's cousin, Dean, from Atlanta with his three children, two of Aaron's co-workers, Charles and Saanvi, Jenna, and Jeff from the foundation. Aaron came in to see how he could help but Mira always preferred to take care of the table herself. Holidays were tradition and tradition mattered to her. She held onto every moment and every memory.

Each year, she invited her guests with the same reminder that they need not worry because she wouldn't be cooking. She hired a chef and a helper to cook, not for herself, she claimed, but as a service to the people she loved. She wouldn't subject them to her attempt at a roasted turkey. As compensation for her lack of culinary skill, she focused on the décor and printed out interesting articles about the holiday for guests to read and discuss at the table. She wanted dinner to be more than just a meal.

There was noise from the kitchen, noise from the bedroom where Aaron was watching sports, noise from the hallway where her housekeeper was vacuuming, and then the wonderful noise of Lilly, out of breath, coming through the front door and yelling "Home!" The sweet sounds of hurried preparation for a holiday dinner filled her with a peaceful happiness. She was dragging a chair across the floor when she had the thought again, *This is the best that life will ever be.*

At two o'clock, she called Willie to make sure he had gotten Mae home and things had gone smoothly. He assured her that all was well. Her father had paid for the ambulette service to carry her up the three flights of stairs to her apartment and she was back in bed, exhausted.

"I made sure everything was ready for her," Willie said. He sent Mira a picture he had taken on his phone of Mae asleep in her room. She noticed that at Mae's bedside was a single yellow rose in a glass. Neither she nor her parents had sent any flowers.

"Thank you, Willie," she said, her usual icy tone having melted a bit. "I will be over tomorrow. I hope the food delivery arrived. Happy Thanksgiving."

Willie reported that it had arrived, and he asked Mira to thank her parents. "We appreciate you," he said. "Happy Thanksgiving to you."

Everyone started arriving at four o'clock. Jenna made a bee-line for Lilly whom she adored.

"Look at this gorgeous girl!" she yelled as she grabbed her and pulled her into a hug. "My God, what a beauty! I am so happy to see you!" Jenna didn't have a daughter and treated Lilly like the future daughter-in-law she only half-jokingly said she wanted her to be. Lilly loved her back and blushed every time Jenna talked about her marrying her son, Gavin, someday. Mira approved of the idea but warned her friend that no child marries the person they are told to marry, so the better strategic move for them both was to pretend that they didn't care either way.

"That she is—gorgeous!" Matt broke in as he entered the room with Dana. Lilly ran to her grandparents, carefully hugging Matt who looked serene at that moment. Then she leapt into the arms of her grandmother.

Mira loved to watch her mother with Lilly. She had a natural ease with her granddaughter that she had never been able to develop with her own daughter. Mira had always assumed close female relationships weren't Dana's "thing," but once she had Lilly, she concluded that, in her mother's case, they just skipped a generation. She wasn't unhappy to see the connection with Lilly even though it bypassed her. Lilly brought something out in Dana that Mira was relieved to know was in her, even if she could never quite feel its direct effects.

"What's the latest with your father?" she asked Jenna, pulling her aside.

"I was there this week. We moved him in."

"Tell me," Mira prodded her. "I know it's a lot and you are doing it all on your own."

Jenna's usually bright demeanor was suddenly dimmer. "You know what I never expected, Mira?" she began. "I never thought it would hurt to think of my father not being here. He wasn't of much use to me in my life, but he was the layer above me, you know? With Mom gone, and him going now, I realize that I am somehow…exposed. Even with him being who he was, and even with him like he is now, he was and is that layer, sort of. I don't know how to explain it better than that."

Mira looked lovingly at her friend. "You don't have to," she said. "I know exactly what you mean."

Aaron's coworker, Charles, walked over and seemed to drift straight to Jenna, as men often did. She brightened instantly. Jenna had an internal, almost reflexive, reaction around men that was more than just charm. Mira always told her that she was constantly giving all men that entered her orbit the attention and affection she would have showered on her father if he had been around. It was a gift that he missed out on, and Mira always thought that if he had only known what it was to be loved and appreciated by Jenna, he would have regretted his behavior terribly. It was his loss, and the rest of the male species were the beneficiaries of his bad choices. Charles was basking in his moment, so Mira greeted him quickly and then went to see her parents.

"I would love to know how you got here," she said to her father. "Did they put you and your walker on a luggage cart and roll you all the way?"

Matt smiled. "I wish we had thought of that," he joked. "Getting into that car without pulling every muscle in my back took twenty minutes, not to mention the toll it took on my masculine pride."

She knew he wasn't really joking, just laughing at the absurdity of the very unfunny condition he always found himself in. But at least he was laughing.

Her father seemed happy to be out and once again at Thanksgiving at her home, the way it used to be. But Mira could see the cautious hesitation on his face. Aaron's colleague, Saanvi, came over to greet Matt and extended her hand to shake his. Mira watched her father raise his arm and work hard to make the movement seem natural, but she knew it was a struggle. He seemed uncertain himself that the effort would produce the desired result, which was not only a simple handshake but the appearance to others that it was no effort at all. She saw anxiety and shame in his eyes in the moments before his hand reached Saanvi's and relief when it did. It wasn't a small victory.

Mira walked with Matt to his chair and helped him get settled just moments before she called everyone else to the dining room to sit down. She knew he wouldn't want others to watch him try to navigate the complicated and hazardous task of getting into his chair. Dr. Baron shuffled in just at that moment and, catching Matt's expression, he quickly pulled his handkerchief out and pretended to sneeze loudly and rub his nose. The brief distraction averted his gaze just as Matt painfully lowered his aching body into his seat, using his two weakened arms and his daughter as his spotter. Dr. Baron's kindness allowed Matt the dignity of pretending his older friend hadn't just witnessed his fragility, and he was grateful. So was she.

Dinner was loud and boisterous, just as Mira liked it. There were debates about politics and stories about Lilly, like when she was five and came to the table dressed as a chicken, not knowing the difference between her fowl just yet. Aaron's cousin had his two daughters recite the story of the pilgrims' first Thanksgiving while his younger son offered sound effects when they talked about the Indians. Dr. Baron was telling Matt about the latest miracle pain-relieving ointment he discovered, and Jenna and Lilly were laughing together like sisters with a secret. Everywhere she turned, Mira saw life and celebration. Dana's rendition of Mae's stuffing was wiped clean from the platter and the whole room smelled of a feast.

Susie Baum was sitting next to Mira and leaned in to quietly ask after Daniel. "Not here I see. Is he having a Thanksgiving dinner with his friends?"

Mira didn't know. She remembered when Daniel was not only at the table but the life of the party. She remembered when he dominated the conversation and made her belly-laugh with his witty one-liners, delivered at just the right moment. Then she remembered that those memories were twenty years old.

There were others. There were more recent years when he sat at the table, sullen. Everything her father said seemed to grate on him. Often, he would get angry and leave the room. Whenever guests were over, Daniel withdrew, and Mira knew why. People asked innocent questions about what he did for a living, and he had no good answer. At twenty, he had the cover of youth. After thirty, he was just humiliated. He started showing up less and less.

"Knowing Daniel, he is out with friends having spaghetti tonight," she said, trying to make a lighthearted remark. Susie simply put her hand on Mira's back and rubbed it gently.

"He doesn't even know how much he is missed," Susie said softly.

As plates were being cleared, the children had grown weary of sitting still and raced off to the kitchen to watch cartoons. Mira looked across the table at her father and recognized an old, familiar expression on his face. He was happy. Every now and then, she caught him wincing from one of the many sharp pains that shot through his leg or back, but, overall, he seemed in good spirits.

Getting him out of his apartment and back out into the world was what he needed. He had managed his food without help, and to someone unaware of his recent ordeal, he might have appeared almost normal in his movement. He even refused Dana's offer to bring him dessert.

"I will get it," she heard her father say. "If I let you go, I will get one cookie crumb and a couple of grapes. I see lemon tart over there and you aren't going to keep me from it," he said as he rose from his chair. It took him two tries, but he managed to swing his upper body forward with enough momentum to allow him to push off the table and rise. His hands steadied him and Mira swelled with optimism at the sight of it.

He left his walker behind and started toward the dessert buffet just a few feet to the side of the table. Just then, the little boy who had been watching television in the kitchen ran through the door, racing away from one of his sisters, laughing. He didn't see Matt and charged full speed into him. Mira saw it all happen, like a car crash occurring in slow-motion in front of her eyes. Her father, startled and destabilized, let out a sound she hadn't heard before as he tumbled back and landed on the floor. There was a loud thud as he hit the ground that Mira felt throughout her entire body.

The boy was scared and ran into the living room. Mira and Aaron jumped up and raced over to Matt. So did Jenna, Jeff, and Aaron's cousin, forming a rescue party around him. Matt had landed on his backside and was in a seated position on the floor. No one wanted to move him until they assessed any potential injury from the fall.

Mira knelt close to him, and the room fell entirely silent, except for the faint sound of Lilly gasping. She looked up momentarily and saw her daughter, wide-eyed, with her hands over her mouth, trying to muffle her cry. She turned back to her father.

"Dad…" she began. Matt was staring straight ahead.

He let out a long breath and then said, "Shaken…not stirred."

Mira ignored the attempt at humor. She continued. "Your back, Dad. Is it okay? Does anything hurt, feel out of place?"

He shook his head. "No," he said softly. "No, nothing. I am okay."

Once she was convinced that he hadn't broken any bones, she thought about the other casualty of the fall—his damaged pride. She wished, absurdly, that everyone would keep talking, and look elsewhere. She knew he wished that too.

"Let's get you up," Aaron offered. He and Jeff gripped Matt under his arms and Mira stood behind her father with her hands at his back. On the count of three, they carefully lifted him to his feet and escorted him to his chair just steps away. Jenna pulled it out so he could easily get in. Matt was pale and still not saying much. He had been scraped off the floor, but Mira could see his dignity wasn't.

"Dad," she said gently, "should we call an ambulance? Just to be safe?" She could see her mother on the other side of Matt's chair now, bracing herself.

"No, thank you, Mira. No, I don't need an ambulance. Thank God, I got lucky. I am overweight. The impact was padded by all those shortbread cookies I sneak in after dinner that your mother doesn't know about."

He was making jokes, which was usually reassuring, but just this once, she wished he wouldn't. She could see that he didn't think it was funny, and she agreed. It wasn't. He had the look of someone who got off the tracks just before the train rushed by. Then that look quickly turned into that of someone who had forgotten for a moment he wasn't a healthy young man of twenty and got a serious reminder—in front of an audience.

The table was silent. It seemed everyone was still holding their breath. Dana walked quickly into the kitchen and returned a moment later with a glass of orange juice.

"Drink this," she said as she handed Matt the glass, her hand now shaking. "Your blood sugar is dropping because of the shock to your system," she said. He obeyed and Mira watched as the color began to return to his face, but the sadness and shame were still there.

Aaron moved quickly to the other end of the table and began speaking loudly about something work-related with Charles, and light conversation began slowly again around the table. The dreadful silence broke. Jenna put her arm around Lilly's shoulders and asked to see pictures of her dorm room on her phone. Mira could see that her father was relieved to no longer be the center of attention or, worse, the subject of pity.

Dr. Baron sighed deeply and looked over at Matt. "Okay, young man," he said, placing his hand on his reassuringly. "Life just never leaves us alone, eh? But we are still here, right? Okay. Okay." He spoke as a senior member of the aged and infirm club to which Matt belonged, and in their shared membership there was the comfort of not being alone. Matt placed his hand on top of Dr. Baron's in gratitude.

Dana then went to the buffet table, took a plate, and filled it with cookies and the lemon tart, and anything else that would fit. She walked it over to Matt and placed it in front of him. "More padding," she said with no discernible emotion in her voice. She simply placed one hand on her husband's shoulder. Mira was fascinated by her mother at that moment.

Mira moved around the dining room trying to make conversation with her guests, but she never took her eyes off her father. She watched his every move and expression. Everyone was kindly asking if they could help. If only someone could, she thought. She couldn't concentrate, so a few minutes later she excused herself and walked into the kitchen.

Now that the shock had worn off, the fury set in. She leaned against the counter to brace herself and lowered her head for a moment before looking up and letting her thoughts go. They came furiously.

Mira raged at a world that seemed designed to infiltrate happy moments with bitter ones. She was bitterly angry at the God her father thanked after being lifted from the floor. He was the God who allowed missiles to nearly miss terrorists in their cars but directed a five-year-old's footsteps straight into Matt Frank at Thanksgiving dinner. It was because of Him that her father was on that floor in the first place, and she silently accused him of inexcusable neglect.

He was the God who made suffering the feature of life, not the bug. Mae praised Him even as she lay wasting away in her bed and Mira wanted to know if He felt any guilt at all about accepting accolades He hadn't earned. What had He done for Mae of late that would have merited another Psalm, another "Thank you, Jesus"?

She cursed old age which seemed to be nothing more than a cruel reminder that Ecclesiastes was right—it was all vanity.

Gratitude for the small things be damned. They were taken away too. She wanted to know why, in addition to all else life took from people, it had to take their dignity as well.

Most of all, she was angry that she had allowed herself to believe that things would get better. Decline may not be a straight line, she told herself, but the trajectory was still downward.

She raged at her kitchen counter for several minutes, trembling, with her eyes closed and her hands clenched tightly. There were no tears. She didn't want to cry.

Once the anger began to process, the awareness that it did her no good set in. Spent, she relaxed her grip and remained still, her eyes still closed. She realized, suddenly, that her bitter accounting of God's world and its failings was more than a tirade, it was a prayer. She had been talking to the God she resented and despised in that moment of fury. She still thought He cared what she felt and was willing to listen. So maybe it had some value after all.

Emotionally drained, she opened her eyes. She turned around and saw the chef and his assistant huddled in the corner of the kitchen, trying to act casually, as if they had not just witnessed her emotional meltdown. She couldn't think of anything to say or do but return to her dinner party.

The little boy peeked through the doorway. He was aware that something bad had happened, and he looked terrified. His father grabbed him up and walked over to where Matt was sitting. "Mr. Frank, I am so sorry," Dean said with his son in his arms, the little boy's head buried in fear and shame in his father's chest.

Matt looked up and smiled. "Don't be," he said kindly. "Life knocks you on your ass every now and then, right, Dr. Baron?"

He brought his fellow traveler through old age and infirmity in on the conversation.

"If only it were just every now and then," Dr. Baron replied, smiling as only someone who had been knocked on his ass by life could. "And look, at least you got an apology. Life doesn't usually give me those," he observed. Matt nodded in agreement.

Though everyone tried their best to enjoy the rest of the meal, Matt's crash to the floor broke up the party. People started leaving and Mira didn't protest their departure. She couldn't smile for another moment. Her father was still in his seat with Dana now sitting beside him. His dessert plate hadn't been touched.

Mira sat beside him. "Dad, you are sure you didn't break anything? Nothing hurts?"

He shook his head. "Just my ego."

"You should take some Advil tonight," she continued. "You are going to feel sore tomorrow from bracing against the fall. Your muscles will ache."

He nodded. "I will, dear," he answered obediently, laying his hand gently on his daughter's. He was still her father and he wanted to reassure her. Placing his hand on hers was all he had at the moment. Mira noted that his hand felt cold and weak, like Mae's.

Aaron helped his father-in-law to his feet and accompanied him and his walker to the door. Mira noticed that he held the handles firmly, his knuckles turning white. Lilly carefully hugged her grandfather and didn't let go for some time. Matt closed his eyes for a moment, released his grip on the walker, and embraced his granddaughter. Mira could see his depleted energy levels being slightly restored by Lilly's warmth.

"I'm sorry," he said to her quietly, "that I ruined the meal. But this hug makes it all better."

Lilly looked at her grandfather. "You didn't ruin anything. And I am sorry that I didn't hug you sooner."

~ ~ ~

In bed that night, Mira dialed her brother. "Hey, sis," Daniel said casually as he picked up.

"Daniel, Dad fell tonight at dinner."

She didn't continue with any detail, waiting to see what her brother's response would be. She wanted a reaction she knew she wouldn't get. She wanted him to apologize for not coming for Thanksgiving, and she wanted a sibling's advice about whether to call his doctor or a specialist. She wanted Daniel to say he would book a flight the next day to New York and that he was just as worried about their father as she was. She wanted an equal partner in the care of her aging parents. She didn't really imagine she would get one, but she called him anyway, because he was her brother.

"Yeah," came the reply, "Mom texted me." Mira let the silence linger for a moment to give him time to say the next thing. "Uh, he seems okay, right?" Daniel asked.

"He does," she replied. "Did you speak to him?" She knew he hadn't.

"No. I will call him tomorrow," he offered. It wasn't the best offer, but Mira knew she had to take it.

She had a million things to say at that moment but made the choice not to say any of them. The prospect of trying to navigate the future without her father and Mae in it seemed unbearable without the support of a brother to whom she could turn. But the prospect of that same future without any brother at all seemed worse. Venting her anger and frustration would only push him further away. So, Mira released her brother from the responsibility of consoling her, hoping that one day he might at least be around to reminisce about when they were children, and tell stories about family vacations. There was no sense in wishing for what was or wondering where it went anymore, she realized. She would accept what was there in front of her, however insufficient.

"Great!" she said as cheerily as she could. "Just making sure you knew. And about Mae too—I am sure Mom told you."

She had. Daniel hadn't called her either. "Does she even pick up the phone?" he asked half-seriously.

"I will call you from there the next time I go," she said.

"You go there to see her?" he asked incredulously.

"All the time," she said quickly. Then it was quiet again. "Okay, Daniel, it's late and I am wiped. Gotta go. Happy Thanksgiving." Her brother hadn't said a single helpful thing, and she didn't want to linger on the phone with him long enough for him to say something that would hurt.

Like her mother, she hung up the phone before he responded.

~ ~ ~

The next morning, she called her father. "How are you this morning?" she asked. "Did you sleep?"

"A little," he replied. A lie, if the sound of his voice was any indication. She could also hear the deep sadness in his words, though he was trying not to show it. She wondered if he could hear her fighting back the tears.

Emotion always came up for Mira after she had processed an event, never in its midst while there was a job to do. Even then, she didn't cry often. Aaron used to tease her that her tear ducts must be clogged up with all that eyeliner she used trying to get the Madonna look in the eighties. Mira simply felt that there was little use for actual tears, and they were best reserved for emergency situations. If he ever saw her crying, she explained to her husband, he would know it was serious.

"Are you in pain today?" she asked her father.

"When is the answer to that question ever no?" he replied lightly.

"Seriously, Dad, come on," she pressed him, her voice cracking. "Nothing? No new pain?"

Matt chuckled and simply answered, "Nothing I can distinguish from all my other pains, so I guess I am okay." Sometimes she wanted to wring his neck.

"You are seriously impossible. Honestly, please, just tell me." She was frustrated now, which was good news because her annoyance had edged out her sadness.

"I am a little stiff and I have an ugly bruise on my leg, but that's it. Really. I really did get lucky. God was good to me."

God again. She wasn't in the mood for Him.

"Dad, is life really this absurd?" Mira asked.

"Well," he replied, "old age certainly is. I wouldn't quite call it a comedy, but it is laughable a lot of the time."

"You know what I was thinking about all night?" Matt said suddenly to his daughter.

"What?"

"Thanksgiving at our first apartment, before you were born. It was a tiny place, and we didn't have a big dining room table. Mom would cook everything, and my job was to go down to the storage room and haul the big folding table and chairs upstairs so we could seat everyone. I used to carry that eight-foot table under one arm and three chairs in the other. I wasn't always like this," he said.

"Of course, you weren't," Mira agreed. She wished she had a memory of her father that way, or an old video. She wanted to see him like that just once. "And maybe you won't be carrying furniture around again, but you won't necessarily get worse either," she offered, lying to herself again, and to him.

"Okay," he said, not wanting to debate the matter.

Mira knew she hadn't said the right thing. But she didn't know what that was anymore.

"I am going to see Mae," she said, changing subjects. "I will video-chat you in when I get there. Then I am going to come back and come over to see you. I will pick Lilly up from your place. She and Mom are painting together this morning."

Matt was quiet again for a moment and then simply said, "Okay, great."

DO NOT FEAR, FOR I AM WITH YOU

WHEN MIRA ARRIVED AT MAE'S apartment, Tracy, the day nurse the Franks had hired, was there. She reported that Mae hadn't eaten much since coming home from the hospital and refused to get out of her bed. She slept most of the time and read her Bible when she was awake. The doctors hadn't found any illness or condition they could treat, but Mae's vitals weren't strong.

Tracy was a kind woman, dressed in light pink scrubs with her hair pulled back in a short ponytail. She spoke with a thick Jamaican accent and the experience of a woman who had been caring for the homebound elderly for twenty years.

"We are just going to make sure Mae is as comfortable as she can be," she said, putting her hand on Mira's arm reassuringly.

When Mira walked into Mae's room, she found her awake in bed, sitting up, with her Bible on her lap. Her head turned toward Mira slowly and she smiled. She seemed half the size she had been just two days earlier.

"Mae, how are you feeling?"

"The Lord is good, Mira," she answered softly. "You've got to praise Him."

Mira felt a lump in her throat as she spoke those words. *Do I?* she thought to herself.

"Dad wants to talk to you," she said as she pulled out her phone and called her father on Facetime. He answered right away, and the two old friends met again. There was no moment of technological fascination and no formal greeting. They just looked at each other, and Mira wondered who would be the first to speak.

"Mae, do you remember when mother and father took me to the synagogue for my bar mitzvah that Thursday morning before school?" Matt began, without bothering to say "Hello." There seemed to be no need to start a conversation that had been ongoing for more than seventy years.

"I sure do," Mae said faintly, her lips hardly moving, but her eyes glimmering with recall of that day so long ago.

"I was nervous," he continued, "and didn't want to read the Torah in front of all the people at the service. I complained to my parents at the breakfast table about having to do it and told them I was never going to do it again after that day."

She nodded, remembering it well.

"You were making me pancakes at the stove and mother asked you to say something to her stubborn son. I remember you put your hand on my shoulder and looked straight at me and said, 'Child, you ain't doin' this for nobody in that there synagogue. You doin' it for you and your God. You goin' to be a man in His eye today.'"

Mae smiled. "Yes, and you did do it, sure enough. Wasn't nothin' you didn't do once you set your mind at it. You were a good boy, Matthew," she said lovingly. "You were always a good boy. And a good man too."

Mira welled up with emotion trying to picture the scene from a New York kitchen decades earlier. In it were a version of her father and of Mae she struggled to imagine—young, strong, and looking to the long, expansive future with hope and expectation. Only Mae could go back there with her father and remind him of what his life was like before he became a man and had to face the world. As he sat in his father's chair at home, now an older man, trying to recover, his greatest source of strength was an even older woman, for whom recovery was no longer an option. The memories he shared with her appeared to have a restorative power. It seemed as if it were possible to momentarily access the vitality of one's youth, just by recalling it together with someone who was witness to it.

They spoke for a long time. The conversation which started so long ago seemed as though it could go on forever. Neither looked ready to hang up, so Mira continued to hold the phone for Mae. She listened carefully to the stories they told and tried to commit as many of them as possible to her own memory.

She wondered if her father would tell Mae about the fall, but he didn't. Then Mae whispered something to Matt slowly, fixing her eyes on him. "So do not fear, for I am with you; Do not be dismayed, for I am your God. I will strengthen you and help you."

Mira didn't recognize the quote. She knew it was one because it wasn't Mae's voice.

"Isaiah," Matt said.

"You've got to praise Him, praise the Lord," she repeated.

"I do, Mae. I am grateful to Him, and to you."

She cleared her throat and reached her fingers out to touch the screen gently, as if she were stroking Matt's cheek. "I'm tired now, Matthew. I'm goin' to say bye now, okay? I gotta go."

Mira could hear her father exhale deeply. "Wait, Mae, wait. Don't go yet."

She smiled at him kindly and the two old friends lingered, looking at each other for a few seconds, saying nothing. Then he spoke. "Yes, it's okay. Goodbye, Mae."

Mira thought her heart would break.

But it didn't. Instead, she got busy after she hung up the phone. She cleaned Mae's room until it was spotless. She couldn't coax her out of bed, but she managed to pull off her old socks and she wiped her feet down with a warm washcloth. She placed new, plush socks on her feet and covered her body with a warm blanket. She cleaned her thick-lensed glasses which she placed gently next to the Bible at her bedside and put water into the small glass with the yellow rose.

She sat next to the bed and lingered as Mae fell asleep. She could hear her low, slow breathing and she touched Mae's hand gently. For a long while, Mira said nothing. She just stayed near Mae, not ready to leave.

When she finally spoke, she could think of just one thing to say. "I am taking Lilly to synagogue tomorrow, Mae," she whispered gently, just inches from her face. She thought that even in her sleep, Mae would hear her, and like what she heard. Then she left the room.

On her way out, she thanked Tracy for taking care of Mae. "Please call me whenever—if she needs anything, okay?" she asked.

Tracy was kind. "I will call you tonight just to update you, don't worry."

Mira smiled, wondering when the last time was that she hadn't worried.

Before leaving, she pulled a box of Faber-Castell graphite sketching pencils out of her bag that the salesman at the art store had recommended. She left it on the kitchen table with no note.

~ ~ ~

Mira arrived at her parents' apartment and found her mother and Lilly in the kitchen. She had heard them chatting from down the hall as she approached. She couldn't make out what they were saying but she noted the ease with which conversation flowed between them.

When she entered the room, Lilly and Dana were standing in front of easels at the window, with beige art smocks on, smiling. They both loved to paint so much that their faces glowed, Mira thought, in a way that could only happen when creativity was being released. The sight of it warmed her after the morning she had just had.

"Hi, Mom!" Lilly exclaimed, bouncing with youthful energy. "How is Mae?"

Mira didn't want to disrupt the happy air in the room. "She is okay. She spoke to Grandpa. Tracy is terrific, and I trust her with Mae completely," she added, looking toward her mother.

Dana put down her paintbrush and studied her daughter's face. "That's great," she said.

"I am going to wash my hands and put this stuff away and we can go…shopping!" Lilly practically sang out.

As she skipped from the room Mira went over to have a look at the canvases. Her mother remained in place as she approached, as if bracing herself. The paintings were portraits they had done of each other.

Lilly's was an astonishingly beautiful picture of her grand-mother as a younger woman. Her hair was silkier and there was a warm, red tone to her cheeks. Mira was suddenly reminded of something she couldn't believe she had forgotten. Her mother wasn't always old either.

Then she looked over at her mother's portrait and felt emotion moving through her suddenly that she couldn't quite place. It wasn't Lilly that Dana had painted, she realized. It was Mira, and her face was troubled and sad. She could feel her mother's eyes fixed on her, but she couldn't bring herself to look over at her. This was how her mother saw her. And it was also, oddly, how she would have painted her mother. Lilly walked in suddenly.

"Wow!" Mira said, happy for the distraction. "These are amazing! Artistic talent clearly skipped a generation in this family!" Her tone was breezy and detached now. "I am so ready to go shopping! You?" she asked her daughter.

"Is that a trick question?" Lilly shot back. The clever comment was a reminder, though she didn't need one, to check in on her father.

"Just going to say hi to Grandpa, and we'll be off," she said, and she went to the living room to find him.

And there was her father, where she seemed to always leave him, back in his father's old recliner. "Someone who can't move around much is always easy to find," she teased him as she walked in. "I guess there is a silver lining to everything."

"Before you ask, I am fine!" he exclaimed looking up and preempting her question. "In fact, I was just about to get up and do a jig."

"Oh, well, lucky me!" she said, playing along. "I have never actually seen a jig and this is my chance!"

He smiled. "Eh," he said, waving his hand, "the mood has passed. Maybe later."

She sat down. "I am okay, really," Matt said with less fanfare, looking straight at her. "Mae seemed…" He couldn't find the word.

"She isn't okay," Mira said, relieving him of the parental task of making it easier on her.

"No," he agreed, nodding, "she isn't."

"So how was the art studio session this morning?" Mira asked.

Matt instantly brightened. "Lilly is such a beauty. Inside and out," he said with genuine affection in his voice. He adored her. "I worry about her!" That was his way of saying he loved her, Mira understood. He worried about everything he cared about.

"Believe me, I know," she agreed.

"She has such incredible talent. Did you see what she painted?" he asked.

"I literally can't believe what she can do with a pencil or a paintbrush," Mira answered.

"I can," he insisted. "She got that straight from your mother. You know, she drew all the time when I first met her. She was always so talented."

Mira nodded. "Yes, you told me, remember? I am still trying to process that one. I wonder why she didn't do anything with it all those years?"

"Maybe being married to me stifled her creativity."

Mira thought at first this was one of his funny one-liners, but she wasn't entirely sure, and she didn't ask.

"Okay, well, we are all still stuffed from last night and no one wants to pick you up off the floor again at another meal, so we are going to have a quiet Friday night dinner at home," she said, hoping it wasn't too soon for that line of humor.

"I don't blame you," he replied approvingly, appreciating the nod to his fall by way of a joke that made it unnecessary to talk about it further.

"And guess where we are going tomorrow morning?" Mira offered. He waited for the answer. "Synagogue. Lilly asked if Aaron and I would take her."

She mentioned it as though it were a line from a comedy sketch that would be followed by a loud funny sound meant to emphasize an unexpected moment. Instead, Matt replied quietly, as though to himself. "Oh, I would love to go to synagogue…."

Something about that wish, and the wistful way in which he said it bothered her. "Don't…" she stopped him abruptly.

He was startled by her reaction. With his eyebrow raised, he looked at her and waited.

She waited too, hoping the urge to say what she was thinking would pass, but it didn't. "Dad, really," she said, taking a deep breath, "you could do so much more. You could go out more and do more things if you weren't so proud! Wheelchairs are not the end of the world. Not going out and living life because you are too proud to use one may be. Go to synagogue if that is something you want to do. Come with us tomorrow. You can't just sit here, in your father's chair."

She paused, hearing the annoyance and judgment in her tone, but unable to stop herself from lecturing him. "People in wheelchairs don't often end up falling to the floor. And they can go to the opera, and to dinner. They can be in the world – maybe not the way they want to be, but at least the way others need them to be."

"Mira," Matt said, answering her calmly, "I can't be the man in the wheelchair whom they park in the aisle next to his family at services. That would be my body there, but not me. I am sorry I can't do that for all of you. Truly, I wish I could. Maybe a stronger person than I am would be able to do it. But I can't. I love you, but please understand, I can't."

Mira instantly felt ashamed. She realized she sounded like her brother, and looked like her mother's portrait of her. She changed her tone. "Dad, there is no stronger person than you," she began to reply. "I just meant…"

He interrupted her again. "Mira, my body has been betraying me most of my life, and old age is a physical betrayal for everyone. I am not going to get stronger, or 'better' in my eighties. What happened to my hands after the surgery was a blow, but I believe I can recover enough to be able to put my own hearing aid in again. That's good enough for me. As long as I am not totally dependent on others…that's good enough. I have traveled all over the world, eaten at the finest restaurants. I have had a very full and interesting life. I don't feel deprived of experiences. I don't really care about those things anymore, and there is no chair in the world that I want to be in more than this one," he said, rubbing the arms of his father's old lounger.

She wasn't entirely satisfied, but her anger was gone. She looked at her father in his chair and knew he meant every word he said. "I know Dad, I just…I just don't want you to give up on life. Whatever that means, I don't even know. But you just can't do that."

Matt smiled at his daughter. "Give up?" he repeated. "No, Mira. I am not giving up on life, just the life I used to have. It isn't mine anymore. All of life is about knowing when to fight and when to let go."

Mira thought he said that last part directly to her.

"Okay, Buddha, that's wise advice. I'll be sure to consider it," she said sarcastically.

Matt rubbed his belly and shrugged. "You won't have a choice." Then he winked at her.

YOU HAVE TO LAUGH...

THAT EVENING, JENNA CAME OVER and sat with Mira, Lilly, and Aaron at the kitchen table for a "Sabbath lite" dinner made up of Thanksgiving leftovers. Jenna wasn't Jewish but one of her stepmothers had been, and she had taught Jenna how to bake a sweet challah that Mira couldn't resist. They sat in their sweatpants around the round, glass table and Mira teased her friend that only she could make an oversized hoodie seem chic. They laughed and ate for an hour before Aaron excused himself and went to watch the game. The girls grabbed their mint teas and went to curl up in the den.

"How is your grandpa?" Jenna asked Lilly. Mira was curious to hear how her daughter would answer and was surprised to hear her respond exactly as she would have.

"He's okay, I think," she started. "Good thing he bounces well for a senior citizen." Lilly looked at her mother as she spoke, checking for her reaction. She and Jenna laughed.

"Yes, a very good thing!" Mira agreed.

"And how is your dad doing?" Mira asked Jenna.

"Well, I spoke to him on the phone yesterday briefly," she began. "Usually, he just listens to me talk and occasionally says one or two words. For the most part, they have nothing to do with what I said. But strangely, all of a sudden, he started talking as though a current had gone through his body and restored his consciousness. His voice even changed. He said, completely coherently, 'Listen, dear, I have to apologize to you.' For a split second, I thought he was having a moment with me. I thought this was my big 'come to Jesus' moment with my father. He was finally acknowledging what a bad father he had been, and he was breaking through his Alzheimer's to deliver the message. I was almost in tears." Jenna spoke with anticipation in her voice, building the story exactly as she had experienced it. Mira and Lilly were captivated.

"And then," she continued, "I was reminded that life is not a Hallmark movie. My father paused and said, 'I wasn't good to you all those years, I know. I am so sorry, Anne.'" She paused as she rolled her eyes and leaned back in her chair.

"Wait!" Lilly jumped in. "Who is Anne?"

"I have no idea! She wasn't one of his many wives. I am guessing she was one of his many mistresses. Of all the women he wronged in this life, Anne is the one that gets the apology! Or, who knows? Maybe Anne was his childhood dog!" Jenna laughed at the absurdity of it all.

"You have got to be kidding me!" Mira said, shocked. "I mean, what do you make of all that?"

Jenna didn't miss a beat. "Sometimes there is nothing to make of life," she answered looking at Lilly. "You just have to acknowledge it and laugh at how ridiculous we all are." Lilly stared intensely at her as she spoke.

Mira looked over at her daughter who seemed riveted. "What do you think, Lilly?" she asked her. "Do you agree with that?"

She turned her head quickly to her mother and smiled sweetly at her. "I don't know, but if you ever return to consciousness in the midst of Alzheimer's to deliver a message, it had better be the code to your jewelry safe."

All three women burst out laughing and Mira felt a surge of great comfort knowing that she would never fully lose her father. Lilly had so much of him inside of her.

SANCTUARY

Saturday morning services at the synagogue started early, but Mira, Aaron, and Lilly arrived at ten thirty. There were three armed guards outside the building who checked their bags as they entered. Inside, two young men in suits greeted them with the traditional "Shabbat Shalom" welcome. Mira understood that they were volunteers from the congregation who provided an additional layer of security by interacting with people as they walked in, sizing them up and making sure they were there for the right reasons. She was suddenly seized by the same sense of vulnerability her father often expressed about the state of the world, now that she stood in his position, as a parent wondering what kind of society her child was inheriting.

They sat together in one of the many empty rows of the sanctuary, as was the tradition in conservative synagogues. The room could easily accommodate five hundred people, but there were fewer than fifty congregants there. The cantor was singing, and his voice reverberated around the room, bouncing off the walls. Mira's spoken Hebrew was rusty, but she remembered every word of the liturgy from childhood. The tunes were familiar and comforting as well. Being there felt like a visit with an old friend she had lost contact with.

They rose for the silent prayer and she looked at her daughter standing next to her with her book in her hands, her long hair hanging like curtains around her face as her head tilted downward toward the text. She could hear Lilly whispering the words under her breath. She was completely focused. She studied her for a moment, marveling at the young woman she was becoming, one far more poised, beautiful, and self-possessed than she ever could have hoped to be at her age.

She watched Lilly's fingers gently glide across the page, guiding her through the prayer, and she thought of Mae tracing the words in her Bible with her aged hands. It seemed fitting to think about the old and the new, the past generations and the future ones, in a place like this. Lilly, feeling her mother's gaze, turned slowly to her, blinked once, and smiled. It was a generous, beautiful smile, Mira thought. She smiled back and felt Aaron's hand squeezing hers. She sensed, as she had before, that life in that moment was as good and whole as it would ever be, and she said a silent prayer of thanks for it, noting that her last "prayer" to God was a less happy one.

The rabbi's sermon was about the holiday and gratitude. Five minutes in, Mira began to tune out. She rolled her eyes in disappointment and boredom as he preached a predictable, deracinated spiritual message she had heard dozens of times in spin class. "There has to be a central office somewhere churning this stuff out and distributing it to rabbis across the country," she whispered to Aaron. He smiled and put his finger to his lips to shush her.

She opened the Bible that was in the seat pocket in front of her, figuring God's words would be more impactful than the rabbi's. The hard cover cracked a bit when she opened it, and the fresh smell of newly printed pages wafted up to her nose. The book clearly hadn't suffered from over-use, and Mira was sad to think that she was one of those absentee Jews who had left it untouched. She thought of Mae, closed her eyes, and said to herself, *Okay, let's see what we get*, as she poked her finger into the pages and opened to the place she chose.

She didn't find the inspiration she was looking for. She had landed in the book of Leviticus on a passage about burnt offerings. She could feel the rage returning. Even this magical practice, which had in the past helped her hold onto the remnants of her faith, was failing, and in synagogue of all places. Everything seemed to be leaving her all at the same time. She closed her eyes to prevent the tears from coming. She didn't want Lilly to see her mother like that. Then, she opened them again and decided to rest on her own resources, rather than rely on a guiding hand.

She flipped toward the end of the book where the prophets were and found Isaiah 40:31: "…but they that wait upon the LORD shall renew their strength; they shall mount up with wings as eagles; they shall run, and not be weary; and they shall walk, and not faint." She silently read this passage to herself. It was one of Mae's favorites. She meditated on every word, hoping the promises of the text would fill her heart there in the sanctuary, seated between her daughter and her husband. She didn't wait for faith to overcome her; she tried strenuously to conjure it up. She couldn't. But she consoled herself with the idea that believing it could have worked was itself an expression of faith, if only a weak one.

Services ended, and as Mira, Aaron, and Lilly left the sanctuary and stepped out into the street, Mira's phone began to vibrate. There were three missed calls from her mother. That familiar panic returned as she dialed her parents' apartment.

"Mira, Mae died this morning," Dana said straight away as she picked up. Mira froze in place and said nothing for a few seconds as she absorbed the news. She needed a moment to let the world shift from its "before" state to its "after."

"She died?" she repeated quietly, as though asking might return a negative answer. Aaron and Lilly each grabbed one of Mira's elbows as she uttered those words, as if to hold her up.

"Yes. The funeral is tomorrow in Brooklyn."

Mira was never going to faint, but the support of her family did hold her up in a way.

"Is Dad there?"

Dana passed the phone to Matt.

"Hello, darling," he said kindly.

"Dad, my God. I wasn't expecting…I didn't think…" Mira paused with no way of ending her sentence. Of course, she had been expecting this very news, but it still felt like a shock.

"Hard to believe, isn't it? A world without Mae," he said, filling in her thoughts.

"Hard to believe," she repeated. "Dad, are you alright?"

"Not at the moment, actually," he answered honestly. "I am not. But I know I will be, Mira. Please don't worry about me. You loved her too. Are *you* okay?"

She scrambled for a witty line, even a joke. She wanted to make her father feel better and worry less about her as well. But there was nothing to say other than the truth. "I'm not okay, either, Dad. But I also know I will be too. Please don't worry about me either."

She knew she was asking the impossible.

"Listen, you don't have to come over today or tonight. Rest. Go home. Mom and I are going to rest too. We will all need our strength for tomorrow."

They hung up and Aaron went into the street to hail a taxi. Lilly linked her mother's arm and put her head on her shoulder. "I can't believe how strong you are, Mom. Nothing takes you down."

Mira smiled. "Well, I guess I can't fall apart now that you've said that."

Then she heard her daughter whisper, "That's kind of why I said it."

A TREE PLANTED
BY RIVERS OF WATER

THE NEXT MORNING, THEY ALL arrived at the Franks' apartment early. Aaron and Lilly waited in the lobby as Mira went upstairs to get her parents. She let herself in and walked toward the kitchen. As she approached, she heard what sounded like soft crying and she hesitated before entering. She cleared her throat loudly to give her father time to compose himself and then walked in. But it was her mother at the table, sitting alone with a cup of coffee, her eyes obviously recently dried.

She got up quickly when Mira entered. "Hi, oh okay, you are here," Dana said in one breath, never making eye contact. "Here," she said, pulling a bowl of fruit toward the edge of the table, "want something before we go?"

She didn't wait for an answer. She went to a cupboard and opened it, searching for something inside. She spoke over her shoulder to her daughter. "We sent flowers to the funeral hall. I hope they came out nicely." She closed the cabinet then, without having taken anything out, and started walking toward the door. "I have to get Dad's seat cushions! I can't forget those. And where is your father anyway? I had better move him along." And then she was gone.

The car ride to the funeral hall in Brooklyn was silent. Watching her father struggle to get into the car with Aaron and the driver helping and two seat cushions to assist made a bad morning worse. There was nothing to say.

Mira leaned against the window looking out as they made their way down the FDR drive. The road was in disrepair and the car jolted with every crack in the pavement. She remembered what being eight-months pregnant in the back of a taxi in New York City felt like. Every bump was torture, sending pain down her sciatic nerve. She couldn't see her father's face in the front seat, but she knew he was in agony. Traffic grew heavy and slowed, sparing him for a moment. Then the honking of the horns began, and Mira understood there would be no peace for her father on this ride.

They arrived at a small white stucco building with an old sign on the front that read: God's Kingdom Funeral Hall. There was one man standing outside with a handful of pamphlets and a picture of "Mother Mae Boyd" taped to the front door. As she and Aaron helped Matt out of the car, the muted sound of high tempo music pounded through the walls—like the building had a heartbeat. The man outside handed each of the Franks and the Caynes a pamphlet and they opened the door.

The music hit Mira like a wave. It was loud, boisterous, and joyful. She could hear the tambourines and the foot-stomping from the anteroom. As they entered the funeral hall, the scene was spectacular. Everything seemed to be moving, except the open casket at the front of the room. Men and women were clapping and dancing in place. Some spilled into the aisles when the holy spirit overcame them. They raised their arms toward the ceiling and spoke in tongues, and praised the Lord, thanking Jesus. Their clothes were colorful, and the women wore hats with enormous brims, covered in feathers and rhinestones. It was a scene of overwhelming energy and a true contrast to the ride over. Never had she anticipated so much life at a service devoted to someone who had just met with death.

A woman approached and guided them to their reserved place in the front row. Mira thought she and her family must have seemed like strange foreigners clad entirely in black, soberly walking down the aisle to their chairs.

"Welcome sister," the woman said kindly to her, extending her hand.

"Hello, I am Mira Cayne, an old friend of Mae's. Or, really, she was like a grandmother to me. She lived with us part time, for many years. She was my father's nanny too when he was growing up. They were so close." She struggled trying to describe who Mae was to her and to her family, but found the vocabulary didn't exist. "Did you know Mae from church?"

"I live in the same building as Mother Mae," she answered, smiling sweetly. "Every Saturday morning my daughter would go over to her place. Willie would teach her to draw and to paint. She loves to draw flowers. Mae would always encourage her, tell her that the Lord had given her a great talent, bless her, and recite Scripture over her. Whenever I came to pick Tanya up, Mae and I would sit and talk for a while. I would come home and just feel happier and better. Tanya too. My husband always said Mae was touched by God."

Mira's eyes watered. "Yes, we always felt that too. "How old is your daughter?"

"She is nine." The woman gestured to the little girl to come over and she approached, holding her father's hand. Mira bent down to greet her.

"Hello Tanya, I am Mira. What a pretty dress you are wearing."

"Thank you," she replied shyly, turning from side to side. "It's my favorite color—yellow."

"I love yellow too," Mira said, winking at her. "I think Mae did as well."

She straightened up and addressed Tanya's parents. "I am so sorry for your loss."

"And we are sorry for yours."

Mira sat with her family as the funeral continued, and debated internally whether to approach the casket or not. She had never seen an open one before, nor had she seen a dead body. She wasn't sure what it would feel like to see Mae's. She sat for some time, half-enjoying the beautiful music and half-wondering if she was supposed to be enjoying it. This wasn't a concert, after all, though it felt like one. She turned and looked at her father whose expression she couldn't read.

Suddenly she rose and walked slowly over to Mae. She felt she had to. She approached carefully, as though any sudden movement might disturb her. When she was an arm's length away, she stopped and looked at Mae's face. She looked exactly as she had the last time she saw her, when she was asleep: small, sunken, like the spirit within her had removed itself and gone elsewhere. Looking at Mae in the casket was like looking at the best possible portrait of her, but not her.

She took two steps closer and reached over to touch Mae's hand one last time. She wasn't sure if she was supposed to touch the body, but she felt she needed to. No prayer or biblical passage came to mind at that moment. No wisdom. All she could think to say was, "Thank you." She whispered it, staring directly at Mae, hoping she could somehow hear her.

The tears welled up in her eyes then, but she fought them back before turning around and returning to her seat. Her father sat almost motionless, a little slouched over, as though some of the life had gone out of him too.

The music continued for another twenty minutes, until the spirit had moved through everyone in the room. Lilly was sitting next to her grandmother who had been expressionless the entire time, her hand tightly holding her granddaughter's. Mira thought to herself that she had never seen such an open outpouring of authentic emotion before. It was an overwhelming sensory explosion.

Then she felt the tears begin to roll down her cheeks. She had been holding them back, but she couldn't any longer. She turned away from her father so he wouldn't see and feel he had to use any of his energy to console her. Instead, she looked at her daughter, determined that Lilly *would* see her mother cry. She wouldn't discover twenty years later that her mother was human. Lilly's eyes welled up as well, and mother and daughter smiled sweetly at each other through their tears. Mira felt she was correcting a small part of her broken maternal inheritance.

Eventually people slowed down. The music followed. They began to take their seats and a small man in a suit and a hat walked to the lectern at the front of the room just in front of Mae.

"Praise the Lord!" he exclaimed.

"Praise the Lord," everyone responded in unison. It brought the entire room to attention.

"Today we come to celebrate our sister, Mother Mae Boyd," he said. "She has gone home, and we thank you, Jesus, for calling her to you! Amen. Hallelujah."

The room responded in agreement, "Hallelujah."

Every sentence the pastor uttered was followed by an affirmation from the crowd. It was an interactive group eulogy. The rhythms of it were well understood by these regular churchgoers who required no prompting to repeat after him or to sit or stand on cue. They knew exactly what to do. When he began a biblical verse, they finished it with him. When he said that Mae was a woman who feared the Lord, they knew to repeat, "She feared Him! Yes, she did. Praise Jesus."

Though Mae had lived in Mira's family home much of her life, she had an entirely different family on the weekends. Her church was her family. Its members spoke her language. They didn't smile sweetly when she spoke in tongues to heal a sick friend. They joined her in the intonations. They didn't marvel at her abiding faith, they shared it. Mira had loved the Mae she saw through her childlike lens, filtering everything through her own experience. Only after Mae's death could Mira see her as a woman. She loved and appreciated her more then.

When he was finished, the pastor turned to Matt and addressed him personally. "I call on you, now, Mr. Matthew Frank, to say a word about Sister Mae. She spoke about you and your family all the time. I feel I know you, and I welcome you to speak today on our sister."

Mira watched as Aaron helped Matt to his feet and over to the lectern. Her father stood at the front of the room and paused for a moment to look at the faces of the people who knew Mae and who were mourning her. Willie, who had been seated in the front row across the aisle jumped to his feet and leaned forward extending his hand. Matt took it and nodded slightly in recognition of him. Neither said a word.

"My family and I are guests here in your church community," Matt began slowly and clearly. "We are grateful to God to be here with you all today, to mourn Mae with those who loved her as we did." He spoke the word "God" with extra emphasis.

The room reacted with shouts of "Welcome, brother" and "Praise God."

Even with his broken body and bruised spirit, her father seemed powerful standing there, Mira thought. He had a presence that people responded to—she most of all. She listened carefully as he continued.

"In many ways, Mae and I shared our lives for the last seventy-four years," he said, seemingly astonished by his own uttering of that length of time. "What moment of importance in my entire life can I think of, that she was not there for? She celebrated with me, and she cried with me. I knew her pain and her joy and she knew mine. She was a constant friend and source of comfort. I hope I was that to her in equal measure." He paused for a moment and took a breath. The room was silent.

"The mysteries of life evade me," Matt continued. "Even at my age, there is so much I don't understand. I cannot explain how a southern, black, Christian woman would come to be one of the most important and impactful people in the life of a white,

Jewish man from New York City. I cannot account for the hardships Mae suffered even as she remained the most faithful and true believer I have ever known. But I know this—God's ways are not our ways." Mira could see nods of recognition on the faces of every person in the room. This was a form of religious acceptance they appeared to have arrived at long ago, and one they recognized immediately when her father acknowledged it. Mae had always known it too, and modeled it for Mira, who struggled still to give in to its essential truth.

"What Mae and I shared most deeply, was the language of faith, taken from our shared traditions, and interpreted through our respective life experiences and struggles. Our battles may have been vastly different, but we fought them with much of the same armor. As I stand here today to remember her with all of you, I can only use that language to describe Mae, her life and what she meant to me. In the Book of Psalms, 'Tehillim' in Hebrew, women like Mae Boyd are best described, 'V'haya K'etz Shatul Al Palgei Mayim.' Mae was, 'Like A Tree Planted by the rivers of water.' The rivers of water that sustained her were the words in her beloved Bible, and those are the only words I can use to talk about her today."

As her father spoke the words in Hebrew, Mira could hear the chain of history clanking behind him. It gave extra meaning and depth to his characterization of Mae that he spoke about her in the language of his ancestors. She was the last witness to all that preceded Matt Frank and it reminded Mira that her father now stood ever closer to the end of his part of the chain in this world. She was heartened to know there was an attachment between those who are here and those who are gone. Chains don't easily break. Then she thought of her brother who hadn't flown in for the funeral. He was part of the same chain, even if he didn't know it, or want it. This made her both sad and hopeful.

She noticed the silence in the room. Several people had raised their hands in the air, as if to receive the spiritual vibrations of her father's words. They reacted to the holy sound of spoken Hebrew as though the energy of the words had been released into the air and their arms were antennae reaching for the signal.

"Mae's love and friendship followed me from boyhood to adulthood and into old age. It is not enough to say I am grateful. In the Jewish tradition, when someone dies, we say, '*May Her Memory Be For A Blessing.*' I hope you will all allow me today to invoke the Hebrew, '*Zichrona L'Vracha.*' May the memory of Mae Boyd continue to be a blessing to others, as her life was to me."

With watery eyes, Matt left the lectern and returned to his seat. Mira reached over and held Lilly's soft hand. She wondered about what her father said and if it were enough consolation to know that such deep loss would be mitigated only by the idea that the memory of the deceased would be "for a blessing." Was that helping her father right now? Would it help her?

There was gentle music as the pastor returned to the front of the room to provide details of the internment. Staff came in, closed the casket, and escorted Mae's body down the center aisle and into the next room. She was gone.

After the service, Mira and her family headed toward the car they had waiting for them outside. She felt a tap on her shoulder and turned around to find Willie standing before her. He tipped his cap as usual but wasn't smiling or effusive as he had always been when he saw her. She wondered if he missed Mae and felt her loss the way she did. She wasn't sure, but she did note there was a solemn look on his face.

"Miss Mira," Willie began, "I wanted to tell you thank you for all you and your family did for Mae." He looked down as he spoke.

"You don't have to thank..." she began to answer him, but he stopped her.

"I know you took better care of her than I did. I know that," he continued reflectively and with what Mira thought was more than a flash of guilt across his face. "I thank God for you because my great-aunt deserved to be watched over the way your people watched over her. I couldn't...I didn't do enough, that's for sure. Not enough. I just wanted to tell you that."

Mira was stunned. She had made so many judgments about Willie and what he did and didn't do for Mae over the years. Maybe he did what he could. Maybe he didn't. How could she know what he had been through or what his challenges were? She really knew nothing about him. As she stood there facing him, she thought about her brother.

"Willie, thank you for saying that," she said softly. "It was my privilege to help Mae however I could. I thank God for that privilege too." There was a moment of mutual acceptance, if not entirely understanding, between them that she knew only Mae could have orchestrated.

Willie reached out his hand and handed her a small brown shopping bag. "These are Mae's things," he said. "I know she would want you and your family to have them." Mira's hand trembled as she gently took the bag from him. The tiny package contained treasures, she thought, as she gripped the handles and smiled warmly. "Thank you," she said looking directly into Willie's eyes.

"You are welcome, Miss Mira," he replied as he tipped his cap and walked away.

She watched him get into one of the cars accompanying Mae's body to the cemetery. She and her family weren't going. Her father couldn't navigate the broken pathways. Willie would be there with Mae and Mira thought she would like that. He was, after all, her family.

She didn't open the bag. She didn't want to rifle through Mae's belongings yet. Mira smiled, though, as she looked at the small sketches of flowers that decorated the plain brown exterior.

The car was quiet on the way home. She thought about the service, the beautiful music, and Mae's small body lying in the front of the room. She thought about her father's eulogy and Willie's words. Mira knew that something more than Mae's life had ended on that November day. A whole part of her own had concluded too.

~ ~ ~

When they arrived at the Franks' apartment, Aaron and Lilly decided to walk home and let Mira spend some time alone with her parents. She went up to their apartment and sat around the kitchen table with them recounting stories about Mae. Some of the tales were so ancient, they seemed like folklore, part of the Frank family oral history.

Then Mira opened the small bag Willie had given her. It contained three envelopes and Mae's Bible. The first envelope had Mira's name on it. She opened it to find an old photograph, yellowed around the edges, of Mae, Matt, and Dana standing together in front of a small cottage-like house in the country. In Dana's arms was Mira at a year old, and in Matt's were two suitcases. They were the hard, rectangular leather cases people used before someone thought to put wheels on luggage. Heavy and cumbersome, they hung from the young Matt Frank's arms in the photo as if they were made of air.

"Where was this?" she asked her parents, tilting the picture toward them.

"My God," Matt exclaimed, "that was taken not long after you were born. We rented a tiny house in Nyack, New York for the summer and took Mae with us. She loved that house. There was a mini strawberry bush in the backyard, and she would pick fresh berries every day and make pies and jam with them."

Dana looked surprised too. "I had forgotten about that place!" she said, enjoying the memory of it. "I can't believe Mae kept this photo all this time!"

Her parents were looking at the house and recalling the summer they were new parents. She was staring at the image of her father with two heavy bags in his hands and creating a new memory of him as a young, strong man with the endless potential of his future in front of him. She loved Mae at that moment more than she ever had for sharing that part of her father's history with her.

The next envelope was addressed to her mother. It contained a note from Willie that read, "Great-Auntie Mae asked me to write this down for you." What followed was the recipe to Mae's famous Thanksgiving turkey stuffing. On the bottom of the page was a charming sketch of a turkey with a blue apron tied around it and a wooden chef's spoon in its hand. Dana showed it to Mira and Matt and then placed it carefully on the table in front of her and gently placed her fingertips over it, smoothing out the corners. She loved Mae too, Mira could now see, and she wondered why she had never seen it before.

The last envelope was for Matt. Mira was surprised because she had assumed the Bible would be for him. Perhaps both were and Mae hadn't left anything for Daniel. She would have to come up with some lie to tell him about that later.

Matt opened his envelope with a bit of effort. His fingers still weren't working perfectly, but neither Mira nor her mother attempted to help him. This was his work to do. When he finally tore it open, two pieces of paper fell out. One was the old worn picture of Mae's son, Joseph. Matt's eyes welled up with tears when he saw it.

"When Daniel started drifting away from us, or when it first became clear to me that he was," Matt said softly, "Mae used to take out this picture of Joseph and pray over it, and over me and Daniel. She used to tell me that her son had gone far away, but she knew one day God would bring them back together. She didn't know how long it would take, but she knew it would happen. She said the Lord would bring my son back to me too, and I just had to keep praying and waiting on Him for His time."

Dana's chin was quivering. Rather than change the subject or make a lighthearted comment, Mira just waited and watched. Her parents seemed to breathe in and out together, absorbing the moment, and she didn't make a sound.

Then Matt picked up the small piece of paper that had fallen on the table and unfolded it. It was the certificate Mae had received from the Jewish National Fund on her fiftieth birthday saying seventy trees were planted in Israel in honor of Ms. Mae Boyd. Matt and Dana had made the donation in her honor, knowing that she would be overwhelmed, and she was. What she couldn't have imagined was that for her seventieth birthday, they would fly her to Israel to touch those trees and see the plaque with her name on it staked into the earth alongside them. Matt often talked about that moment and Mae's profound reaction to it, as a devoted Christian woman standing on the land of the Bible. He described it in detail—the expression on her face and the sounds she made as she said, "Thank you, Lord" and stood, planted in the earth like one of her holy trees. He always described that day as one of the most important spiritual moments of his Jewish life.

It felt like the perfect time to pull Mae's Bible out of the bag and hand it to her father. As Mira drew it from the bag, she saw a piece of white paper sticking out of the pages with two words on it: "For Daniel." She was arrested in place with the Bible clutched in her hands. She slowly turned the book toward her parents so they could see the note. Matt's head bowed and he simply said, *"Zichrona L'Vracha."*

~ ~ ~

The next morning, Mira and Aaron slept in. It was ten o'clock, and they were still lying in bed with the newspapers, emotionally exhausted from the funeral. Mira felt that starting the day meant starting the new chapter of her life without Mae in it, without the last person in line before her father. She decided all of that could wait a few more hours.

She turned to her husband and asked him a question she had never thought to ask him before. "Do you ever talk to your parents, Aaron?"

Aaron considered the question. "All the time," he answered. "I will say out loud, 'Mom, please watch over Lilly at school,' or

'Dad, thanks for teaching me how to play tennis. Everything you taught me, I taught my daughter.' Stuff like that. So yes, I guess I am 'talking' to them, but honestly, I don't know if I am talking to them or to myself."

He looked at Mira sweetly. "Do you think it matters which it is?" he asked her.

"No, I guess not. I suppose it is only important if they start answering back." She winked at him.

She was relieved that he didn't just answer her the way he was supposed to, but with honesty and uncertainty. Those seemed like the two most important things he could offer her as they sat together trying to absorb something beyond anyone's understanding.

She reached over to her nightstand and picked up Mae's Bible. She was holding onto it until she could hand it over to Daniel. She wasn't sure when that would be, but she liked having an important piece of Mae still with her.

At noon, Mira and Aaron stood with Lilly at the front door, kissing her goodbye. She was heading back to school.

"Well, this was definitely not a boring weekend," Mira said half-heartedly trying to make some kind of a joke.

"Yeah, if I come home for Christmas break, can we just order pizza and watch Hulu?" Lilly answered, playing along.

"What do you mean, 'if?'" Mira said in mock horror. Aaron kissed his daughter on the forehead and Mira grabbed her and held her close. "I ain't stuttin' 'bout you, child," she whispered in Lilly's ear. "You are coming home for break, or I am going to show up in the hotel room next to yours wherever you go," she teased her.

"Mom, is Grandpa going to be okay?" Lilly asked, looking to her mother for assurance.

"Of course," she said.

"I can't believe Mae is gone," Lilly continued, holding her mother's hand. "I mean, I knew she wouldn't be here forever, but I thought we had until just before forever. Does that make sense?"

She held Lilly's face in her hands and looked into her eyes. "Perfect sense," she answered.

SOME PEACE AND A
LITTLE LIP BALM

MIRA WALKED SLOWLY OVER TO her parents' apartment. There was bumper-to-bumper traffic along Fifth Avenue and the honking cars made an overwhelming amount of noise. *There is no peace in this city,* she thought. Just then a taxi driver leaned out of his open window and spat on the ground before pounding the door of his car with his open hand and yelling at the driver in front of him to move, even though there was nowhere to go. Mira walked faster, abandoning all hope of collecting her thoughts.

She let herself into the apartment and walked down the hall to find her mother sitting alone in the living room. Dana looked up as her daughter entered.

"Hi," Mira said, noting the silence in the house. "Is Dad here?" She didn't mean to be rude, but she realized that she sounded that way. To correct her mistake, she sat down across from her mother.

"No, Gloria took him out for a walk around the block," Dana answered. "He needs to start moving around more." Mira nodded in agreement.

There was a long pause and Mira felt uncomfortable. She didn't know exactly what to say to her mother. As she struggled, Dana uncrossed her legs, leaned her elbows onto her knees and drew in toward her daughter. She was looking directly at her now. Mira squirmed a bit in her seat. She hated not knowing exactly what to say or do at any given moment. Her mother always seemed less bothered by awkward silences than she was.

"Your father isn't going anywhere any time soon, Mira," she said plainly to her daughter. She said it definitively, the way Mae used to make divine pronouncements.

Mira looked away. "I know," she said softly, unpersuaded, and surprised to find that her mother understood her deepest fear.

"He can't," Dana repeated. "He is needed too much here," she said. Then Mira realized she and her mother had more in common than she had realized.

Gloria's loud voice at the door interrupted them. "I didn't come in on Thanksgiving weekend to listen to your nonsense!" she was yelling, clearly addressing Matt.

"No, you came in because you can't live without me!" Mira heard her father reply. "Women have always been unable to resist me," he continued as the keys jangled in the lock. Dana smiled and rolled her eyes.

"You're not even my type," Gloria retorted. "I like blondes."

The sound of her father doing what he did best was wonderful and reassuring.

"You just can't admit how much you love being around me," he teased her as they entered the living room.

Matt brightened when he saw his daughter. "This old broad just had the thrill of her life walking me around the block," he said with a smile, pointing at Gloria and winking at Mira.

Gloria just waved her hand and laughed. "Only old person I see is you!" she laughed. Mira laughed too. "And just so you know," she said as she left for the kitchen, "I have had much bigger thrills in my life than walking you around."

Matt sat down in his father's chair opposite his daughter. He let out a series of short, sharp breaths and then a long one, as though he had just run laps around the block. For him, the brief stroll was an effort. Gloria returned with a glass of water. He took it from her, and his weak arm shook under the weight of the full cup, but it held. That was progress.

"Thank you," he said to her as she began to walk away. "But if you had really wanted to help you would have brought me a cookie too."

Gloria turned around as if to banter back, but instead she pulled two shortbread cookies out of a napkin from her pocket and placed them on the table next to Matt. She put one hand on his shoulder and softly said, "If cookies will help, then today you get two."

Matt looked at his daughter. "I don't know what helps," he said, reaching for a cookie, "but I know that shortbread never hurts."

Mira had wondered if her father would be different now. She wondered if Mae's death would be the death of her father as she knew him. But that one cookie reassured her that while so much had changed, he was mostly the same.

There was a brief silence. Nothing seemed worth saying. Then Dana turned to her daughter and said, "Daniel called this morning. He was so sad about Mae."

Mira stiffened. She heard the excuse-making in her mother's voice and the sound of it was insufferable. Daniel hadn't been sad enough to call when Mae died, or to fly in for the funeral. But he called the next day, and his mother felt the need to highlight the gesture, even if it was the very least he could do. She tried to avoid eye contact with her father as she struggled to resist the overwhelming urge to say what she felt. She leapt up and grabbed the second cookie Gloria had given Matt, shoving it entirely into her mouth to make an outburst impossible. She nodded politely as though impressed by the crumbs of compassion her brother had thrown at his family and kept chewing.

Dana looked at Matt and then at Mira and lowered her eyes to her folded hands in her lap. She sighed as though in resignation, and addressed her daughter in a tone of voice Mira hadn't heard from her mother before. "Daniel should have come in for the funeral," she said simply. "He should have, but he didn't. Maybe he…couldn't."

Mira turned to look at her mother now, and she could see how difficult the words were for her to utter. She could also see that her mother wasn't saying this for herself, but for Mira—and that she couldn't go any further. Mira released the tension in her shoulders and allowed them to drop. "Yes, maybe."

Dana rose to her feet and said she was going to go lie down, and she left the room.

Mira swallowed the remainder of the cookie and turned to her father. "Well, you were strangely silent," she said to him, trying to elicit some reaction.

"What is there to say?" he replied. "I have no idea what happened to Daniel or why he runs from our family the way he does. All I do know is that one day, he will come back."

She knew what her father meant by "one day" and she shivered at the thought of it. She had spent so many years dreading the moment he wouldn't be there anymore. Ironically, her fear had always been that the person with all the answers wouldn't be there to help her find them. Now he was admitting he didn't have them himself. It felt like time for a joke.

"Maybe you and Mom should have another child," she declared. Matt looked at her, intrigued. "Maybe the next one will stick around and help me out a bit when I need it," she teased. Matt smiled and waved his hand.

"I can't afford another child!" he laughed. "Financially or emotionally."

"Dad," she said, interrupting their lighter moment, "can I ask you something? Why is it so important to you that Daniel say *kaddish* when you are gone?" It occurred to her that while there were many questions he couldn't answer for her, there were some that he still could.

"Your brother doesn't really know me as an adult, Mira," he answered. "He probably won't before I go. When I am gone, he will regret that. If he says *kaddish* for me, he will know that he was bound to me by thousands of years of tradition and faith, and that will console him. Some sons can't reconcile themselves to their fathers in life. Some need to do it when they are gone. I want to help him with that. I want it for him, not for me."

Mira wished Daniel understood how much his father loved and worried about him. Maybe that would only happen once he was gone.

"'Gone.' Dad, you keep saying 'gone,'" she changed the subject from trying to understand her brother, to what she wanted to understand for herself. "Where are you going exactly? Where do you think that is? Where do you think Mae went?" She wasn't exactly sure why she asked. Maybe she wanted an address for her silent prayers or maybe she wanted to know what her father really thought about death, aside from all the preparations he seemed to be making for it.

Matt bowed his head a little, as if to acknowledge his lifetime of pondering that same question and the weight of knowing there can be no certain answer. But then his head lifted again, and he looked perfectly content when he answered his daughter. "I don't know. No one knows," he said. "But I will be happy just to have some rest."

"Rest?" she repeated. "That's the best you can hope for? Not a bright light and harps playing, and your childhood dog running toward you across a verdant field?" Mira teased him.

"No, just a body that doesn't ache, and some peace."

She strained to think of anything better to wish for her father than an existence with no pain, and real peace, but she couldn't come up with anything.

"Well," she answered him, "that sounds like a reasonable request. But do me a favor and before you completely float away on a cloud, can you promise to come back just once and haunt me, just so I know you are still there?"

He smiled, enjoying the thought. "Sure!" he exclaimed. "Happy to. But I think we need to work out a signal, right? Butterflies, or flashing lights—something like that—so you know it is me."

Mira thought for a moment. "How about a code word—maybe, lip b-a-l-m," she suggested. "When I hear someone saying it exactly that way, I will know it is definitely you."

"Perfect," he answered, laughing. "Deal."

On the way home she called Daniel. He didn't pick up. She usually never left messages on his voicemail but this time she did.

"Hey, it's me. Call me when you can. Remind me to tell you a funny story about Dad and lip balm. I miss you."

~ ~ ~

Mira arrived home and went straight back to bed. She had expected everything to be entirely different today, but it was all eerily the same. Aaron came in and handed her a bowl of mint chocolate chip ice cream and sat on the edge of the bed beside her.

"How are you?" he asked.

"Never better!" she said with sarcastic enthusiasm.

He gently squeezed her hand and instructed her to eat. "Few things are as clear as the emotional and spiritual benefits of ice cream in moments of difficulty," he said. "Sometimes sugar is the answer you have been looking for."

She smiled. "I literally think that may be true," she answered as she began eating.

"How was your Dad?" he asked, getting up and walking toward the door.

"Unbelievably, he was mostly the same. Harassing Gloria, worrying about Daniel, joking around—the usual. He didn't even mention the fall, or the funeral. It was my Mom who surprised me."

Aaron turned around to face Mira. "Really? How?"

"She seemed more…present. I am not sure."

"That's a good thing, right?"

"Yes, I guess so."

He smiled and stood in the doorway looking at her. "I think it is. I think it is a step forward."

"I suddenly need to watch a great old movie," Mira said abruptly, as she turned on the television, preferring for the moment, to look backward.

When Aaron saw Spencer Tracy on the screen he winked at his wife. "You have seen this one at least five times," he said. "You know the whole story already."

"Exactly," Mira answered, curling up under the covers as Aaron left the room.

Mira didn't feel herself falling asleep, but she woke up an hour later to a quiet room. She reached over to retrieve Mae's Bible. She caressed the cover of the book and took a moment to breathe in the lingering scent of Noxzema.

"Mae," she said aloud, "I have been using your Bible like a Ouija board. Instead of looking for answers, I should be looking for meaning. Forgive me for getting that wrong all this time."

Mira paused and laughed at herself, but she still had more to say, even if Mae wasn't there listening. She looked up because it seemed to be the general direction of the deceased and added, "I am going to give this to Daniel like you asked. Time for me to buy my own. It won't be the New Testament—I know you understand. But every time I read my Bible, I will think of you." She waited a few seconds for a flashing light or a butterfly to suddenly appear, just in case. Then she laughed at herself again.

THE SAME BUT DIFFERENT

ON FRIDAY NIGHT, MIRA AND Aaron arrived at the Franks' apartment for Shabbat dinner. They met the Baums in the lobby and went up together. Dr. Baron was already there, and so was the smell of Mae's brisket wafting out of the kitchen. Daniel wasn't there, and so everything seemed just as it had before Mae died, except for Mira herself.

Before they sat down, Susie Baum pulled her into a corner of the room. She spoke softly and held Mira's hands as she looked directly into her eyes. "How are you holding up, darling?" she asked with great compassion in her voice.

"I am okay."

Susie stroked the top of Mira's hand which she held in hers. "Mae was very special, Mira. I know how important she was to you and your family."

"Yes," she agreed, "I am not really sure what a world without her in it looks like. And of course, Dad is holding it together, but he has to be suffering…"

Susie nodded and then quickly added, "And your mother. She suffers too."

Mira nodded. "Yes, she does."

Susie's voice broke as she continued. "As I get older, Mira, I feel closer and closer to my son. I am catching up to him now,

I can feel it." She looked serene as she talked about seeing Andy again. Mira gripped her hand tighter. "We all need to feel we are moving toward something as we get older. Age takes so many things away. Your mother needs that too."

Mira thought Susie was very kind to worry about her old friend this way. "Daniel will find his way back to us," she reassured her. "I know my mother is heartbroken over him. I know she is struggling to reach him, but I believe things will be better." Susie's eyes never left Mira's as she answered her. "Mira, darling, it is you she wants to reach." Mira knew it was true, but she didn't know what to say. She hugged Susie and they walked together to the table.

~ ~ ~

Mira sat next to Dr. Baron throughout dinner and when dessert was served, he reached over and took her hand kindly. "I was sorry to hear about Mae," he said gently. "She lived to a ripe old age."

It was a curious comment, she thought, and one Mira had heard thousands of times before. Was "ripe old age" necessarily a good thing? When people said it, that seemed to be what they meant. Were Mae's last years of life "ripe"? Were her father's? As she held Dr. Baron's aged hand, she felt little "ripeness" in its shrunken, fragile structure. Why did people wish for such old age?

She must have winced because Dr. Baron's eyes widened a bit. He noticed the confusion on her face. "Mira," he said looking straight at her, "you know I am something of a pioneer of old age in my family. My parents each died before their seventieth birthdays. My mother's parents and siblings were all killed in the war and my father was an orphan and only child. I never knew what old age would look like for me because I never saw it in the people closest to me. But I am ninety-two years old now. I have been old for a while, and I have been paying close attention, and do you know what I have learned?"

She was wildly interested to hear his answer. "What?" she asked intently.

"All of life is a confrontation," he said. "You confront adversity, disappointment, yourself, your nature, God, the consequences of your choices, relationships, and everything else life puts in front of you as best you can. While you are young and healthy, try to teach yourself how to confront everything with purpose, dignity, humility, and hope. And of course, an iron will, the will to fight. If you practice all that while you are young and strong, you will have a storehouse of everything you need to confront getting old. The challenges can be cruel, but you will have had eighty-or-so years to prepare to take cruelty on. The only old people I know who are terrorized by old age are the ones who spent their early years avoiding, escaping, lying to themselves, or giving up. They aren't trained for battle. Those are the old people I pity, not people like Mae, or your father."

He spoke slowly and clearly, the way wisdom is meant to be spoken. Mira held his hand a moment longer.

"Thank you," she said, her eyes smiling at him now in admiration and appreciation, "for not telling me that old age is a state of mind, or that the inner wisdom you gain compensates for the bone density you lose."

Dr. Baron chuckled. "Oh, dear," he replied, "nothing makes up for going bald and having to give up every food group that ever gave you pleasure. Old age is a pain in the ass. But so am I, thanks to decades of practice. So, it's a fight and I am in it. We'll see who wins."

"What are you two talking about over there?" Matt interjected. "Dr. Baron, you are leaning in awfully close to my beautiful daughter. You know she is spoken for," he teased.

"I wish I had the desire to hit on young girls," he retorted.

"I have the desire to hit on them," Matt shot back, "but what would I do with them once I got them?" He gestured with his weak arms which rose about six inches off the table.

"Alright, alright," Mira interrupted. "I am going to need a team of Austrian psychiatrists to undo all the awful mental images you are both planting in my head right now. Let's move on. We were talking about old age."

Matt laughed. "My favorite subject!" he declared. "I am a world-class expert."

Mira thought she might be one by now as well and it made her feel better.

REFUGE AND A
FINAL REMINDER

THAT SUNDAY MORNING, MIRA LEFT the apartment earlier than usual and jumped into an Uber. As she rode uptown, she felt nervously excited. There were waves of Jewish guilt too. *Good Jewish girls don't go to church*, she told herself, even as she drew closer to her destination—the Greater Refuge Temple on Adam Clayton Powell Jr. Boulevard in Harlem.

The night before, she and Aaron had been talking about Mae, her funeral, and that wondrous music. "That must be what goes on in churches all over every Sunday morning," he said out loud. She thought he must be right. She looked online and found a large Pentecostal church just twenty minutes away by taxi and thought, *why not?*

But as she drew near the building, she began to list the answers to that question in her head. She didn't know if she was dressed appropriately, or what appropriate even was for Sunday morning service. She was worried everyone would know she didn't belong there or wasn't singing along or kneeling at the right moment. She wasn't a Christian—there was that. Was it insensitive to treat their prayer service like a show she was going to watch? Then her grandmother came to mind. If anything would get that woman to return from the beyond one more time, just to shake her finger at her granddaughter, it might be this. All that raced through Mira's mind, but the real concern was that she would go to the Greater Refuge Temple and not find what she was truly looking for—a connection to Mae.

She arrived just before the eleven o'clock service was to begin. She saw a tour bus parked on the corner and understood she wasn't the only spectator showing up that day, and it eased her mind. The exterior of the building was painted in multicolored vertical stripes. It reminded her of a Yaacov Agam sculpture but with a large golden cross in the middle.

When she walked inside, a tall man in an eggplant-colored, three-piece suit greeted her at the door and showed her to a seat in the third pew from the back. Mira sat down quietly where instructed. Just then, the group from the tour bus began to enter and was shown upstairs to the balcony, where the "visitors" were. Mira was relieved to have come in before them and secured her seat in the main hall. She wanted to have the authentic experience, surrounded by regular churchgoers, like Mae had been.

The service had not yet begun but the dozens of purple upholstered seats on the stage were starting to fill up with church leaders. To their right was a large area where members of the choir were sitting and chatting with one another. They were dressed in long choir robes and looked like a professional singing group. Off to the side of the stage was a large, clear screen behind which was an elaborate set of shiny drums. Soaring up the ceiling, at the back of the stage, was a large stained-glass window.

The first several rows of pews closest to the stage were already completely full. There sat the church ladies, as Mira had always imagined Mae to be. They were dressed exactly as attendees at

Mae's funeral were dressed. The hats were colorful and ornate. Their attire reflected the importance of the occasion, showing respect for the church and for themselves. No one was in head-to-toe black, the uniform of Mira's Upper East Side world. Some of the women clutched the hands of young children. The girls had bright ribbons and barrettes in their hair and the boys were in proper suits, pressed and formal.

Her eyes were darting everywhere, taking everything in. Then, a man with white hair and a short white mustache to match his white clerical collar walked to the pulpit in the middle of the stage and announced that prior to starting prayers, worshippers were invited to give "testimony."

An elderly woman with shocks of gray hair sticking out from underneath her small, navy, felt hat rose from the front, right section of pews, and with her Bible in her hand said, "Praise the Lord!" to announce herself as the first "witness." The crowd responded with "Praise the Lord," and the woman began to speak.

She talked about the difficult week she had, suffering from pain in her back and legs, struggling to get out of bed every day. She said she prayed each morning to Jesus, thanking him for his healing, believing for it. Just that morning, she told the crowd, she was able to get out of bed and get dressed and come to church. "My God is a healing God," she declared. "He is a good God," she exclaimed, giving testimony to His power and strength.

"Hallelujah!" some yelled with hands raised into the air. "God is good all the time," others said, agreeing with the old woman's testimony.

Oh, hello, Mae, Mira thought to herself smiling. *Yes, I am here. I am in the right place.*

One after the other, people rose to testify. Each spoke of a specific act of God to which they bore witness that week. No one claimed to have been cured of cancer, or to have won the lottery. Every testimony was to a small act, a small miracle. Each one was appreciated and applauded by a room full of believers who saw God working in their lives every moment of every day. Just like Mae.

After several minutes, the pastor walked back to the pulpit, the organ began to play, and the service started. The pew where Mira sat was now full. Her neighbors to her left and to her right politely greeted her with, "Welcome, sister" and a smile. No one seemed to wonder what she was doing there, and she no longer did either.

The pastor spoke softly at first as he greeted everyone. He pointed to the balcony and acknowledged all the visiting groups, which, as it turned out, were from all over the world. He listed the countries—Brazil, Japan, Canada, Germany. "Brothers and sisters, you are all welcome here and we are blessed to have you with us," he said.

He then asked everyone to open his or her Bible to chapter five of the Book of James (NIV) and to read aloud together. The sound of hundreds of books opening in unison, and pages turning together echoed throughout the room. There were no Bibles in the pews. Everyone had brought his or her own. Mira imagined all those books looked just like Mae's, worn from use. The ownership of the text struck her, especially in contrast to her experience at synagogue where rigid, unopened Bibles sat idly in the seat pockets.

The congregants recited the verse in one voice, as though they had done so a thousand times before. "Is anyone among you in trouble?" they started. "Let them pray." People everywhere threw their hands into the air to receive the divine invitation. "Is anyone happy? Let them sing songs of praise."

Now everyone was on their feet. A man with long hair pulled back in a ponytail, wearing a tan suit, leapt from his chair on the stage and the music began. He turned toward the choir, which was swaying and clapping to the beat, their long robes wafting around them. He led them as they sang, "The Lord Will Make a Way Somehow." Mira rose too, lifted from her seat by the energy in the room. A heavy-set woman with a kind face stepped forward from the choir line and began to sing. Her voice was transcendent, filled with pain and hope. Sixty more voices joined hers and the sound was overwhelming.

People spilled into the aisles and began to stomp their feet and move in fits of ecstatic passion. It was an entirely uninhibited eruption of praise. Nothing about the experience was contained. The choir conductor was waving his arms and jumping up and down as the room shook. Everyone sang along. This was not a spectator sport. Tambourines were everywhere—Mira noticed the congregants had brought those with them too. It seemed to last for hours though it was likely just a few minutes. They were glorious minutes.

When the song ended, several men and women lingered in the aisles, speaking in tongues and dancing in place. They had gotten the holy spirit in them and needed time to return to themselves. The pastor yelled "Amen" and "Hallelujah" as others returned to their seats, and the remaining enraptured worshippers worked through the last moments of their spiritual excitement.

When it was finally quiet, the pastor mopped his forehead with a handkerchief, and made a warm and funny remark about this being a high-octane temple. Everyone seemed to be recovering in their seats, fanning themselves, as he started his sermon. He spoke about choosing God.

He spoke slowly and directly, as if to each congregant personally. "You are going to have to make up in your mind," he told his worshippers, "that for God I live and for God I die." Scattered acknowledgments of "Amen" could be heard across the room.

He cited the Bible throughout his talk. Many of the textual references he made were recognizable to Mira from the Old Testament. She heard their Hebrew translations in her head as he offered them in English. So much of the experience in the church was foreign to her, but at the same time, so much was grounded in the familiar.

When he finished speaking, he closed his eyes, blessed the room, and prayed for healing and hope for everyone in the church, and for everyone around the world in need of God's guidance. Mira wondered who wouldn't be on that list. His final words were, "Trust in the Lord. He will cover you. Praise the Lord, for He is deserving of praise. Amen. Hallelujah."

An organ played softly as an older man in a three-piece gray suit was helped up from his seat on the stage and escorted to the pulpit. It was evident he was a respected member of the community by the way others nodded with reverence as he passed them. He said nothing. He simply paused at the microphone, looked out across the room, opened his mouth, and started to sing.

He sang about the Jordan River in a low, deep, aged voice that filled the entire sanctuary. To Mira, it felt like a generational offering—the wisdom and experience of an elder passed down through the story of a song. He sang about deliverance across a river as though he were having a private audience with God right there in front of hundreds of onlookers who were rooting for him, and he for them. Mira was moved, and at that moment, she missed Mae deeply.

There were more testimonials, more Bible verses, and more electrifying choir music and dancing in the aisles. It was ninety minutes of unrelenting power and praise delivered in alternating waves of rapturous excitement and soothing soulfulness.

She stayed for the entire service. At the end, the educational director invited everyone to the lower level for Bible class immediately following the closing prayer. Mira thought for a moment about going but decided against it. She determined, instead, to call her synagogue the next morning and inquire about classes they offered. It was time to discover her own faith again, not rely on that of others. She knew Mae would approve.

She lingered for a moment at the back of the church before she left. She looked everywhere, and breathed in deeply, with great appreciation for everyone and everything at The Greater Refuge Temple. She had gotten what she came for. Mae was in that room with her.

It was cold outside when she walked across Adam Clayton Powell Jr. Boulevard to hail a cab. Fifteen minutes passed before she could find one and by the time she did, her ears were half-frozen and she was shivering. Desperate to get into the car, she rushed through the door and heard a loud tear. Her coat had caught on a protruding piece of sharp metal and ripped halfway up the back.

She climbed in and leaned back in the seat, resigned to the idea that everything, even a happy morning like the one she just had, would always be a little bit broken. Life didn't tolerate "perfect" very well. That realization didn't upset her as much as it used to.

She leaned her head back and closed her eyes. From now on, she only had memories of Mae and those would have to be enough. She decided they would be, because they had become so deeply a part of who she was, and because she could share them with her father. Mae's memory would be for a blessing, she told herself, because she would use it that way.

Just then, her phone lit up and began to vibrate. She saw her mother's name on the screen and paused before answering. She took a deep breath and spoke.

"Hello? Mom…?"

ACKNOWLEDGMENTS

SPECIAL THANKS TO MIRANDA DEVINE, who is not only a talented journalist and writer, but a truly kind human being. When she offered to introduce me to her publisher, I had no way of knowing she was one of those rare people who would follow through. Miranda, thank you.

Anthony Ziccardi, you went with your gut, and I hope I have made you happy that you did.

Caitlyn Limbaugh, your help made the book better. Thank you not just for your editing skills, but for caring about this story.

Mom, thanks for staying in good health. Keep it up! I don't intend to write a sequel.

ABOUT THE AUTHOR

Jackson Seeley

REBECCA SUGAR IS A WRITER whose column, The Cocktail Party Contrarian, appears in *The New York Sun* every other Friday. Her work has also been published in the *Wall Street Journal*, the *Washington Examiner*, *USA Today*, Spectator USA, Jewish News Syndicate, the *Christian Post*, the *Jewish Journal*, and more.

Rebecca holds a BA in literature from University of Pennsylvania and a master's degree in history from Jewish Theological Seminary. She lives in New York City with her husband, her teenage son and daughter, and her English Bulldog, Batman.